BADLANDS
RANGE WARS

Also by Eldridge James and published by Catnip:

Death in Drygulch

BADLANDS
RANGE WARS

ELDRIDGE JAMES

Catnip

CATNIP BOOKS
Published by Catnip Publishing Ltd
14 Greville Street
London
EC1N 8SB

This edition first published 2010

1 3 5 7 9 10 8 6 4 2

Cover photo of Billy Joe by butterworthdesign.com
Additional background photo and chapter illustrations from iStockphoto

A CIP catalogue record for this book is available from the British Library.

ISBN 978-1-84647-102-5

Printed in Poland

www.catnippublishing.co.uk

For Albert
from Grandpa

CHAPTER 1

'Get your hands in the air! Keep your guns on 'em, men! If they move, shoot 'em!'

The four boys stared in shock at the man in the light brown suit and the two cowboys pointing pistols at them.

'What's goin' on?' demanded the tallest boy, thirteen-year-old Jess, angrily. 'We ain't done nothin'!'

'I said put your hands up!' snarled the man in the suit. 'I want those hands where I can see 'em!'

'What in tarnation is going on here?' demanded another voice, equally angry.

They all turned and saw the lean figure of Sheriff Nolan stomp towards the tumbledown shack in the back alley of Drygulch.

'Sh-sheriff!' appealed Shane. 'The M-Mayor says he's gonna shoot us, b-but w-we ain't d-done nothin' wrong!'

'No one's shootin' anyone!' snapped the Sheriff. To the two cowboys pointing their pistols at the boys and the black and white dog, he ordered, 'Put those guns away right this minute, 'fore I arrest you!'

'They're here with me on legal business, Sheriff,' said the man in the brown suit, Mayor Redding. 'They got a right to carry arms.'

'Carryin' arms is one thing. Threatening boys with 'em is another.' He glared at the two cowboys, Bart and Ben Morton. Both in their late teens and neither of them very bright. 'Bart and Ben, you should be ashamed of yourselves, holding guns on boys like these,' he told them firmly. 'Put them away!'

The two cowboys pushed their pistols back into their holsters. Both of them looked slightly shamefaced.

'We didn't know we was gonna be holdin' up these here kids, Sheriff,' said Bart. 'The Mayor told us he wanted protection from dangerous people.'

'And these boys are dangerous!' retorted Redding. 'Especially that Injun!' he added, pointing at eleven-year-old Billy Joe Ford. 'He's a natural born killer!'

'I ain't no Injun, nor a killer!' Billy Joe spat back, although neither were quite true. He moved towards the Mayor, his fists clenched, his face a scowl of fury. 'See!' said Redding, hastily backing away from Billy Joe.

Nolan caught hold of Billy Joe by his shirt.

'Hold on, Billy Joe!' he commanded. 'No one lays a finger on anyone till we get to the bottom of this!'

Billy Joe scowled, but stopped. He glared at the Mayor and then, as the Sheriff released him, moved back to join Jess, Shane, Andy and Patch.

It wasn't that Billy Joe was ashamed of being half-Indian on his Comanche mother's side – it was just that many people treated Indians as lesser people. As thieves or cheats that weren't to be trusted. It was his Pa, John Ford, an Irishman, who'd been the thief and cheat, and it had got him shot dead right here in Drygulch three months ago. Since then, Billy Joe had become part of the small gang of orphan boys who lived together in a tumbledown makeshift shack. They eked out a living doing odd jobs at the livery stable, at the corral, the hardware store, the saloon. That was the creed that Jess, the leader, had told Billy Joe when he first met them. 'We live right and don't cause no one any trouble. We don't steal and we don't beg. That way the people in this town know we're OK.'

And being a killer . . . he wasn't exactly proud of that.

The Mayor scowled at the boys and at the Morton brothers. Then he produced a wad of papers tied up with red ribbon from an inside pocket.

'Like I say, Sheriff, I'm here on legal business!' he spouted. 'This here's the Deed to these properties, which includes the shack these boys have been infestin'.'

Nolan looked at the boys' shack, and the two buildings on either side of it. The shack the boys lived in looked like it was about to fall down. The two neighbouring buildings were already in a state of collapse. Some of the timber walls had slipped down, leaving gaping holes, and the roofs of both were gone.

'Mr Squires, the owner of the land and the buildings that are on it, died last week leaving some pretty big debts to the bank. Accordingly, the bank is now the owner of these buildings, and it is my job to recover that debt. So we are gonna pull down these buildings and sell the land.' Redding produced another document on thick yellow legal paper. 'This here's a Court Order giving me authority as owner of the bank to take possession of the land and remove any unlawful occupants.' To the boys, he added: 'That's you. I'm kicking you out.'

CHAPTER 2

The boys looked at one another, shocked. They weren't just a gang, they were more like . . . family. And the shack was the place that kept them together. It was their home.

Billy Joe had been running with the Drygulch gang a while. At first there had been Jess, Pete, Shane who was nine, six-year-old Andy and Patch the dog, but Pete had been killed, shot dead. He'd been eleven – the same age as Billy Joe, and Shane's older brother. Now there were just the four boys and the half-deaf dog.

Jess was their leader – the eldest and the tallest, with dark hair parted in the middle, hanging over his long, pale, serious face. Shane was completely different, shorter and stockier with fair hair and a broken nose. Then there was little Andy, who lived in turned-up dungarees held up round the middle with a bit of knotted string and his constant companion, Patch.

They were all strays that had come together for help and stayed that way to survive. Now the Mayor was threatening that.

Andy glared at the Mayor defiantly.

'This is our home!' he protested. 'We live here!'

'Not any more,' said Redding. 'You were never living here legal in the first place,' he sneered. 'And I don't even know why I'm botherin' to talk to a kid like you!'

'Mr Squires said we could stay here,' challenged Jess.

'But you never paid any rent.'

'That's c-cos Mr S-Squires said we d-didn't need to,' said Shane. 'He s-said so long as w-we d-did it up and l-looked after it an' s-stopped it f-fallin' down, th-that was g-good enough f-for him!'

'Well Mr Squires is dead now and he don't own the property no more,' said Redding. 'The Bank does, and I want you out of this place right now.'

'Wait a minute,' put in Nolan. 'Don't they have a right to notice? You can't just turn up and put 'em out on the street.'

'Yes I can,' said Redding. 'They ain't never paid rent, so they're squatters. They ain't got no rights at all. I can either turn 'em out now, or I can pull the house down around their ears. And you, Sheriff, will have to back me up when I do it, because this is all perfectly legal; and you are an Officer of the Law.'

'That I may be, but I draw the line when it comes to

makin' innocent children homeless,' snapped Nolan. 'Hear this, Mr Redding: you may be right by the Law, but when people hear what you've done to these boys there's gonna be some righteous anger in this town. And some people may get so angry they may decide to take their money out of that bank of yours and put it someplace else.'

'My bank is the only one in town,' snapped Redding. 'They got no choice.'

'That might change pretty soon,' said Nolan. 'I hear a new bank's startin' up over in Bluerock. Maybe people might find it worth their time to travel there to do their finance, if they don't like the way you do business. Remember, lots of people in this town have reason to be grateful to Jess and the boys. If it hadn't been for these boys most folk in this town would be dead.'

'The Sheriff's got a good point, Mr Mayor,' added Bart Morton. 'My pappy was saying that same thing just the other day. About how Jess and the boys saved this town from those outlaws.'

Redding scowled and glared at the Sheriff.

'All right,' he growled. 'To show that I'm not just a man of business, but also have a heart . . .'

'A heart!' burst out Billy Joe scornfully. 'You got a yellow streak runnin' down yer back, that's what!'

'Billy Joe,' said the Sheriff warningly. 'Let's keep this calm without name-callin'.'

'As I was sayin',' continued Redding, giving Billy Joe a nasty look, 'because I'm aware of the predicament of these poor orphan boys, I'm prepared to be lenient and give them till this time tomorrow to look for alternative accommodation.'

'This time tomorrow!' repeated Jess, shocked.

'That don't sound very lenient to me, Mr Mayor,' said Nolan. 'Twenty four hours don't give much time for them to find somewhere else to live.'

'It's the best I can do,' said Redding. 'In the circumstances, considering the bad attitude these boys have always shown towards me, blatant and public contempt, they should consider themselves lucky.'

He turned to Jess, Billy Joe, Shane and Andy and waved the legal documents at them. 'You've been warned. I'll be back here tomorrow afternoon, and if you ain't gone by then, I'll have you thrown out.' He looked at the Morton brothers, who were both looking uncomfortable. 'If these two fools ain't prepared to do the throwing out, there's plenty more who will. And it's legal, Sheriff. So don't get any ideas about interferin'.' He gestured at the three ramshackle buildings. 'And if the boys won't leave – these buildings are still comin' down. If they're still inside and get hurt when that happens, then it'll be all their own fault.'

With that, Mayor Redding turned and stalked off, heading back towards the Main Street. Bart and Ben

Morton looked guiltily down at their boots, then at the boys and Sheriff Nolan.

'Sorry, boys. We really thought it was goin' to be a proper bodyguardin' job we was doin',' said Bart, apologetically. They turned and headed off.

The boys looked at one another, the shock of the announcement still sinking in. Jess looked appealingly at the Sheriff.

'Ain't there nothin' you can do, Sheriff?' he asked. 'This is our home?'

Sheriff Nolan gave a sigh.

'Sorry, Jess,' he said. 'I can demand to look at them papers the Mayor was wavin' around, but my guess he's made sure they're all legal like.'

'But where are we gonna stay?' asked little Andy, and the others saw the small boy's lower lip tremble as he fought to stop himself from crying. He knelt down and put his arms around Patch. 'This is Patch's home! He's been here longer than any of us!'

'I sure am sorry,' said Nolan. 'I'll ask around and see if anyone can put you up for a day or two. The trouble is, most people don't have the room for four boys.'

'And a d-dog,' said Shane. 'We g-gotta have P-Patch with us. He's one of us.'

'I know,' nodded Nolan sympathetically. 'But, like I say, all four of you together . . .'

'We ain't splittin' up,' said Jess firmly.

'That's easy said, Jess,' said Nolan. 'But four boys

and a dog is askin' a bit much. I might be able to put two of you up in the jail, while the cells are empty . . .'

'We ain't splittin' up,' Jess repeated, even firmer. 'Thank you, Sheriff, but we'll think of something.'

'OK,' said Nolan. 'But, in the meantime, I'll ask around and see if I can come up with anythin'. But for now, my advice is, start packin'.'

With that, Nolan touched the brim of his hat and walked away.

The boys stood in gloomy silence. Andy hugged Patch tighter.

'W-what are w-we gonna d-do, Jess?' begged Shane, helplessly. 'Th-this is our h-home!'

'We find us a new one,' said Jess confidently.

'How?' asked Billy Joe. 'Didn't you hear what the Sheriff said? No one's gonna take us all in.'

'We ain't askin' to be taken in,' said Jess firmly. 'We're gonna do what we've always done. We're gonna work to make a roof over our heads.'

'Where?' asked Billy Joe.

Jess frowned.

'That I'm still thinkin' about,' he said.

CHAPTER 3

Packing his possessions was the easiest thing for Billy Joe. All he had were the clothes he stood up in, along with a spare pair of old and worn jeans and another shirt. When the clothes he was wearing got too dirty, he took them off and wore the others while he washed the first set. And so on. His real problem was boots. He only had one pair. He kept looking for an old pair of boots he could have as a spare, but so far he hadn't found any in his size. They were either too big, or too small. But he kept looking.

There was one thing Billy Joe did have that he kept a secret from Jess and the other boys. It was a pistol and he kept it hidden inside an old rag, beneath his pillow on his bedroll.

He'd picked up the pistol during the massive gun battle in Drygulch a few months before, when a gang of bandits had taken over the town. He'd taken it from the Sheriff's gun rack during the fight. After that time, when Pete had been shot dead and the other boys had been almost killed, Billy Joe had vowed he would never go unarmed ever again.

The pistol was a Colt 45 with a revolving chamber that held six bullets. It was loaded now. Billy Joe couldn't see the point in not having a gun if it wasn't loaded. If you pointed a gun at someone it meant they were trying to harm you. An empty gun wouldn't stop them. A loaded gun might.

The reason he kept the pistol secret was because Jess didn't like the boys carrying guns. Jess said that it was people who carried guns who got shot the most. But Jess had been badly shot during that gun battle three months before. A bullet had shattered his left leg and it had taken a long time for the bone to knit and mend. Even then, it hadn't mended properly, Billy Joe could tell by the way Jess limped when he walked fast. And when it rained he suffered bad pain from the ache in his leg. Jess did his best not to show it, but his friend could tell.

'B-Billy Joe?'

Billy Joe's thoughts were interrupted by Shane standing by him, a worried look on his face.

'What's up, Shane?'

'D-do you believe in g-ghosts, Billy Joe?'

Billy Joe frowned, wary. The truth was: yes and no. His mother's people, the Comanche, did, and sometimes he did. But his Pa had told him there was no such thing as ghosts. 'When you're dead, boy, you're dead, and that's an end of it,' John Ford had told him.

'Sometimes, Shane,' he said. 'Why?'

Shane hesitated, then blurted out, 'I was th-thinkin' about P-Pete.'

'What about him?'

'If he's a g-ghost, he only knows us as bein' here, at the shack. If we go aw-away, h-h-how will he know w-where w-we've gone?'

Gently, Billy Joe laid his hand on Shane's shoulder.

'Pete will know, Shane,' he said. 'They say ghosts stay around the person they care for most, not the place. Wherever you go, Pete will be there with you, watchin' out for you.'

Shane's face brightened up.

'I-is th-that really so, B-Billy Joe?'

Billy Joe nodded.

'That's what I heard tell,' he said.

It wasn't true. Billy Joe hadn't heard that at all. The main thing was to make Shane feel better.

'Well I guess that's my stuff all packed,' said Jess.

He hefted the roll of bundled-up clothing in his hands. By his feet was a small bag with a few personal belongings in it, mementoes of his life before the gang. He'd actually given Billy Joe one of his most precious possessions: the Stetson hat that Billy Joe wore had been given to Jess by his father.

'I'm n-nearly ready,' said Shane. 'I just g-gotta p-pack my books.'

Shane was the only one of the boys who could read. Read properly, that is. Jess and Billy Joe could pick out a word or two, but only words like 'hardware store' and 'livery stable' and other signs they saw posted up around town. Shane could read words on paper and in books. He had four books, all of them dog-eared with worn covers: one was a Bible; one was a book with maps in; one was a story about some backwoods hero: the thinnest book was a story book with pictures that Shane used to read to Andy. It was about a crocodile. None of the boys had ever seen a crocodile, but the pictures sure made it look a fierce creature.

'So, you thought about where we're goin' yet, Jess?' asked Billy Joe.

'Yep, I think I got me an idea,' said Jess. 'Mrs Johnson's sister and her family come out from Chicago about two months ago to start ranchin'. They're called the Ambersons. They got a spread out on the plain. I remember Mrs Johnson tellin' me they're lookin' for hands.'

'I guess they're lookin' for men, not boys,' Billy Joe said doubtfully.

'We are men,' said Jess. 'Small men, maybe, but we can do any job a man can do. Shane and I can ride and we can handle horses cos of us workin' at the livery stable.'

'But . . .' began Billy Joe.

'And I hear the Ambersons are having big trouble getting ranch hands.'

'Where d'you hear that?' asked Billy Joe.

'From Shane,' said Jess.

Billy Joe looked at Shane, who nodded.

'I h-heard it being s-said at the l-livery stable. There's this big cattle rancher out on the range, Colonel M-McVie, and he don't want no one workin' for the Ambersons.'

'Why?' asked Andy.

'B-because his c-cattle graze the range. The Am-Ambersons are p-putting up f-fences on their l-l-land. This M-McVie don't want fences on the r-range. S-says he'll sh-shoot anyone who tries.'

'So, my guess is the Ambersons will be glad to have anyone workin' for 'em,' finished Jess.

Billy Joe thought it over, then he nodded.

'I guess it's worth a try,' he said. 'Where's this ranch of theirs?'

'Near Blue Ridge,' said Jess. 'About fifteen miles outa town.'

'That's a long way,' piped up Andy. 'How we gonna get there? Patch can't walk all that way.'

'I'm pretty sure Mr Pedersen will let us borrow his buckboard and a horse,' said Jess. 'That way we can take all our stuff with us when we go callin' on them.'

'Say the Ambersons don't want us workin' for

them?' asked Billy Joe, still not entirely convinced by the plan. 'That's a long way for us to go just to come back again.'

'They will,' said Jess confidently. 'We're good workers.'

CHAPTER 4

Next morning Jess went to see Mr Pedersen at the livery stable and told him their plight and their plan. The old owner gladly gave Jess a buckboard and an old black mare called Ruby to take the gang out to the Ambersons.

'Keep 'em as long as you like, Jess,' Mr Pedersen told him. 'I wish there was something more I could do for you boys.'

'Lendin' us the buckboard and the horse will be just fine, Mr Pedersen,' said Jess. 'We'll bring it back just as soon as we're settled in at the Ambersons.'

'You spoke to Mrs Johnson abut goin' there?' asked Pedersen . 'It's her sister, after all, and she could put in a good word for you.'

'I know she could, Mr Pedersen, but you know the way we work: we prefer to do our own askin'. That way we don't owe anyone.'

'Ain't nothing wrong in owing anyone, Jess, so long as they're good people,' said Pedersen. 'And this town sure owes you boys for what you did.'

Jess gave a rueful smile.

'Pity the Mayor don't seem to agree with you,' he replied.

'The Mayor!' snorted Pedersen, and he spat onto the ground with distaste. 'How that man gets himself elected I'll never know!' Then a thought obviously struck him, because he said to Jess, 'One more thing before you go.'

With that he went into the hut that served as his office and came back a moment later with a rifle.

'Take this with you,' he said.

Jess shook his head.

'Thank you, Mr Pedersen, but I'm not big on guns.'

'You may not be, but there are plenty of folk who are, and not all of 'em good. There are dangerous people out on the road. And you'll be passing through Indian country to get to Blue Ridge.'

'The Indians ain't givin' no trouble,' said Jess. 'They're peaceful.'

'They're peaceful only at the moment,' insisted Pedersen. 'If things take a turn, then they won't be.' He grinned. 'Anyway, you could always shoot yourself a jack-rabbit with it if you get hungry on the way.'

Jess looked at the rifle in Pedersen's hands doubtfully.

'I don't know, Mr Pedersen . . .' he began.

Pedersen's face took on a firmer expression.

'Jess, you're taking my buggy and my horse,' he said. 'If you run into trouble I could lose them both. Part of the deal is you take this rifle with you to keep you, my old Ruby and the buggy, safe.'

Jess nodded and smiled, and took the rifle.

'OK, Mr Pedersen. I'll do that.'

'Keep it stashed under the front seat so you can grab it up quick if you need to,' advised Pedersen.

'I will,' said Jess. 'But let's hope I don't need to.'

Two hours later the buckboard had been packed with the boys' meagre belongings. Jess was at the reins, with Billy Joe sitting next to him up front. Shane was in the back with Andy and Patch.

'Your job is to make sure Andy and Patch don't do nothin' silly like standin' up near the edge,' Jess told Shane. 'We don't want them fallin' out and breakin' their neck or somethin'.'

'W-will do, Jess,' Shane assured him.

'OK,' said Jess. 'Let's go.' And with that he let off the handbrake, flicked the reins with a softly called 'Yo!' to the old black mare, and the buckboard moved off, jerking and rattling. They were off to start a whole new life.

✳ ✳ ✳

The horse was strong and they covered the first few miles at a good pace. In the back of the buggy Shane watched Drygulch disappear behind them as the wooden buildings receded into the distance.

Up front, Jess and Billy Joe looked at the vista before them. At first the vast plain beyond Drygulch was desert and scrub: a dusty yellow plain with green plants forcing their way up through the dry, crusted ground, just cactus and brush, but after a few miles it became grassland. To start with, the grass was thin and sparse, but gradually it became a deeper green and thicker – good land for grazing cattle and horses. The road they were on cut a dusty track through the green fields.

Directly ahead, in the far distance many miles further on, the mountains seemed blue, which is how they had come by their name of the Blue Mountains. The lower line of mountains and hills that climbed towards them were known as Blue Ridge.

'They say this is Indian country, but I ain't never seen any out here,' commented Jess. 'Not livin', anyhow. Travellin' and on their way somewheres else, yes. But not stayin'.'

'They're here,' said Billy Joe. 'In the valleys headin' towards Blue Ridge. Least, that's what my Pa told me. But then he lied all the time. Wouldn't surprise me find out he lied about that as well.'

They travelled on and the landscape rolled past

them: grassland, rocks and the distant blue mountains. It was a huge open land beneath an endless sky, with nothing to mark it except the dusty unmade road they were on. In the distance they saw cattle. There were just a few at first, then more and more.

The herd was enormous. The huge beasts, mostly brown in colour, had long sharp horns. They grazed, seemingly unconcerned by the boys in the buckboard as it drove through the herd.

'I s-sure wouldn't l-like to g-get on the end of th-those horns!' commented Shane. 'They'd s-spear someone s-sure as a arrow!'

'So long as nothin' spooks 'em, they're fine,' said Jess. 'Just make sure you keep a tight hold on Patch. We don't want him jumpin' out and barkin'. That'd start a stampede for sure, and that'd be the end of us.'

Jess kept the buckboard moving along at a reasonable pace, the horse trotting and the buckboard rocking and bumping. Billy Joe studied the cattle with a feeling of concern. He'd never been happy around cattle. They were big and strong and they couldn't be controlled. If a dog went mad and started running at you, you stepped out of the way. At the worst, you shot it. If a steer went mad and started running at you, every other steer in the herd joined in. With all that weight and those horns with their sharp pointed tips, you'd either get trampled or run through. Either way, you were dead.

Even against a gunman, you had a chance, because you could try talking your way out of trouble. There was no use trying to talk to a steer.

The buckboard bounced and jerked over the open grassland, until they came to the first of the fences. It was made from wooden fence posts hammered into the ground, with wire strung between them.

'Guess we must be gettin' near the Ambersons' place,' commented Jess.

Billy Joe sighed.

'It sure do seem a pity to fence in somethin' so big and beautiful,' he said.

'It'll never be fenced,' said Jess. 'People can put up fences all right, but the country itself ain't never gonna be fenced in. It'll always be ready to break out.'

In the distance they could see figures near to the fenceline.

'People an' horses,' murmured Billy Joe.

'I count three horses and two people,' said Jess. Then his eyes narrowed. 'No, I'm wrong. It looks like those two are kickin' whoever's laying on the ground.'

'You reckon one of 'em's Mr Amberson?' asked Billy Joe squinting ahead.

Jess frowned.

'Mrs Johnson never said anythin' about her brother-in-law bein' a violent man,' he said. 'I got the impression he was a peaceful kind of fella.'

'Well if he ain't one o' them doin' the kickin', could

be he's the one gettin' kicked,' muttered Billy Joe.

'You could be right,' said Jess, his frown getting fiercer. He flicked the reins and gave a 'Yaah' at Ruby, who picked up speed, taking them faster towards the scene.

CHAPTER
5

As they got nearer they could see that the two men were definitely kicking and punching a third man who lay on the ground near the wire fence. When the boys could see better, Shane suddenly shouted from the back of the buckboard:

'Th-that's Mr Amberson's h-horse!'

'Are you sure?' called Jess.

'Y-yes!' nodded Shane firmly. 'I s-seen it in the l-livery s-stable. That wh-white blaze on his h-head and four wh-white s-socks.'

'Then I guess this is a good time to introduce ourselves to our new employer,' said Jess grimly.

Jess flicked the reins again and the buckboard started rocking and jumping over the uneven ground as they sped up.

'Th-that's Mr Amberson all right!' added Shane, now he could see the man on the ground more clearly.

The sound of the wheels of the buckboard and the horse's hooves made the two cowboys turn towards the newcomers. While one of them stayed beside the fallen Amberson, his booted foot planted firmly on Amberson's body, the other stood and looked at the boys as the buckboard pulled up.

'Get away from him!' called Jess.

His voice was firm and calm, but inside he was tense. He hoped that the men would give up and move on, rather than carry on beating up Mr Amberson in front of witnesses. But the looks on the faces of the two cowboys told Jess this wasn't going to end so easily.

The cowboy nearest them just glared back at Jess.

'This ain't no business of yours,' he said firmly. 'So why don't you kids just move on and go to wherever it is you're goin' to?'

The man on the ground stirred and tried to rise up, but the other cowboy shoved down with his boot, pushing the man back painfully to the ground.

'I'm afraid we can't do that,' said Jess.

While keeping his eyes on the cowboy and a forced smile on his face, Jess was already reaching down beneath the driving seat to where he had stashed Mr Pedersen's rifle. In case of emergencies, Mr Pedersen had told him. He guessed this could be classed as an emergency.

The cowboy spat into the dust and laid his hand on the butt of his gun in its holster.

'I don't think you heard me right,' he scowled. 'Now I'd advise you to get on your way before I'm forced to shoot you.'

'I'm sorry you feel that way about it,' said Jess. And then, with a speed that surprised both cowboys, Jess had snatched up the rifle from beneath the seat and levelled it at the two men.

'I'd better warn you, I'm a pretty good shot,' lied Jess. His voice stayed calm, but inside his chest his heart was hammering.

The cowboys gaped at Jess in shock. The second cowboy was the first to recover. He began to laugh.

'He's just a kid, Mack,' he said. 'A kid with a rifle. Plus there's only one of him and two of us. He can't shoot both of us.'

'Guess you ain't very good at countin',' said Billy Joe evenly.

The two cowboys looked, and saw that Billy Joe had taken a pistol from his bundle of belongings and was now aiming it straight at them. Billy Joe saw the look of momentary surprise cross his friend's face before Jess turned his attention back to the two cowboys. For a moment the cowboys looked stunned, then the second cowboy sneered.

'They're both bluffin'! I ain't gonna be chased off by two kids!'

'Billy Joe ain't bluffin',' chimed in Andy. 'He shot a man stone dead not so long ago cos he was threatenin' us!' He grinned with delight. 'He got him right between the eyes!'

The two men looked uncomfortable at this and they stood, not knowing what to do. They exchanged uncertain glances, then Mack spat on the ground again. He looked at the injured man on the ground and shrugged.

'I guess our job here's done, anyhow, Sandy,' he said sourly. He began to walk towards the horses tethered by the fence. 'So I guess we'll just be in our way.'

'Not so fast!' snapped Jess. 'Stay where you are and put your hands up.'

The two cowboys stared at Jess, bewildered.

'And just what you plannin' on doing with us, kid?' demanded Mack. 'You goin' to arrest us?'

'What I ain't plannin' on doin' is letting you walk away with your guns so you can shoot us as soon as our backs are turned,' said Jess. 'So get your hands in the air!'

Reluctantly, the two cowboys lifted their hands up above their heads.

'Shane, take their guns,' said Jess.

Shane climbed down from the buckboard and moved towards the men, keeping a close watch for any sudden movement on their part. He took their guns from their holsters. All the time, the two cowboys kept their eyes on Jess and Billy Joe, their expressions grim.

'You boys have just made yourself some serious enemies,' grated Mack. 'I'll remember you. Next time it ain't gonna be so easy.'

Shane now had the men's guns and he put them carefully in the back of the buckboard.

'All right, guess you can go now,' said Jess.

The two men put their hands down. They both looked like they wanted to kill Jess there and then.

'This ain't over, kid,' growled Mack at Jess.

The other cowboy, Sandy, turned to Billy Joe.

'The same goes for you,' he threatened.

With that, the two cowboys walked to their horses, mounted them, and rode off.

Jess put the rifle back under the seat of the buckboard and jumped down. He limped over to where Amberson was struggling to sit up. Amberson had blood on his chin from his bleeding nose and mouth, and cuts on his forehead. He was also rasping for breath as he tried to sit up, clutching his ribs.

'Steady,' said Jess. 'Billy Joe and Shane, can you help me load him into the back of the buckboard?'

While Shane jumped down to help, Billy Joe hesitated, his attention on the two cowboys riding off into the distance, the pistol still held firm in his hands. He didn't trust the men not to suddenly turn and launch an attack. But they kept riding.

Billy Joe pushed the pistol back into his roll of clothes beneath the seat and joined Jess and Shane.

Together they got Amberson to his feet, but it was a tough struggle because Amberson was a very big and heavy man. When he had made it to his feet it took all three of the boys to support his weight, leaning on them as he limped and staggered to the buckboard.

Patch was jumping around excitedly in the back of the buggy, and Andy hung onto his neck to stop him leaping up at the injured man.

'Easy, Patch! Easy!' said Andy.

'Thanks, boys,' croaked Amberson. 'I don't know what would have happened if you hadn't come by. I think they might have killed me.'

The boys eased him onto the wooden boards of the buckboard. Amberson pulled himself on board, right into the centre, where he crashed face forward with the effort.

Jess untethered Amberson's horse from the fencepost and fixed its reins to the back of the buckboard.

'Shane. Andy. Your job is to make sure Mr Amberson stays safe in the back there,' Jess ordered. 'And Andy, keep Patch off him.'

'Patch only wants to lick him an' make him better,' protested Andy.

'Mebbe so, but the way he's hurt, that dog jumpin' all over him is only gonna make him worse. So keep Patch off him.'

Jess and Billy Joe returned to the driving seat and

clambered aboard. Just before Jess flicked the reins, he turned to Billy Joe and said, 'Billy Joe, we ought to talk about that gun of yours.'

'The gun that just saved our lives?' asked Billy Joe, pointedly.

Jess looked uncomfortable.

'I still think we ought to talk about it,' he said.

'I only keep it for emergencies,' responded Billy Joe. 'I don't carry it for show.'

Jess sighed.

'You shoulda told me you had it,' he said.

'Why?' asked Billy Joe. 'You'da just told me to get rid of it. Or you'd have told the Sheriff an' he'da taken it off me.'

'Guns are dangerous.'

'Not as dangerous as not havin' one,' said Billy Joe. 'If we hadn't had that rifle of yours and my pistol here, those cowboys woulda shot us all dead.'

Jess shook his head.

'I don't believe that,' he said.

'The only reason you can say that is because we're alive. And we're only alive because we had those guns.' He grinned. 'You were pretty handy with that rifle, Jess!'

Jess shook his head again.

'I ain't gonna argue with you now, Billy Joe,' he said. 'We'll talk about it later. Right now, we gotta get Mr Amberson home.'

Jess whistled and flicked the reins, and Ruby moved forward, hauling the buckboard rocking and juddering behind her, with Amberson's horse trailing after it.

'We can talk about it later, but I ain't getting' rid of it,' announced Billy Joe firmly. 'This here gun just saved my life.'

'We'll talk about it later,' said Jess again, his tone just as firm.

CHAPTER 6

They travelled another three miles before they saw the Amberson house set to one side of the road. As they neared the place, they saw that it was still only partly finished. The timber walls had been put up and the roof was on, but it was obvious from the huge amount of tree trunks and lumber stacked around that there was still a lot more building to do.

As the buckboard neared the house, a woman and two children came out. The woman wore a long blue frock and a scarf tied around her head to keep her hair back. The boy and girl looked like they might be about nine years old – the same age as Shane. The woman, who Billy Joe guessed had to be Mrs Amberson, was smiling and waving in greeting as the buckboard approached. Then she saw the horse hitched to the back of the buckboard, and her expression changed to one of shock. She began running to meet them.

'That's William's horse!' Billy Joe heard her cry out. 'What's happened to William?'

Jess pulled the buckboard to a halt as Mrs Amberson reached them.

'It's OK, ma'am,' said Jess. 'He's in the back.'

William Amberson forced himself to sit up in the back of the buckboard. Even though it was obvious to everyone that he was in pain, he forced a smile. With the dried blood caked around his mouth, it made him look menacing.

'I'm OK, Becky,' he said. 'It ain't as bad as it looks. I just had a bit of a run-in with a couple of McVie's men.'

He tried to get up, but a pain in his side made him wince.

'I think he may have busted a rib,' said Billy Joe.

'He looked even worse when we found him!' said Andy excitedly. 'He was lying on the ground and he looked like he was as good as dead. It's lucky Jess and Billy Joe had guns or we'd all have been dead for sure.'

Mrs Amberson gave Andy a nervous look as she and Jess helped Mr Amberson get down from the back of the buckboard, then supported him as he limped into the house.

'You go in with 'em, Shane,' suggested Billy Joe. 'Mr Amberson knows you. Me an' Andy and Patch'll stay out here till things get sorted out. We don't want to make the place feel too crowded, otherwise they won't want us.'

Shane nodded and hurried into the house.

Andy and Patch had jumped down from the back of the buckboard, and Andy was following as the dog went sniffing around the outhouses and buildings.

'He's huntin' fer rats!' said Andy proudly.

Billy Joe sat down on the steps of the wooden porch. He kept his bundle of possessions with him, near his feet, the pistol hidden inside once more. That pistol had just saved his life. From now on he was going to make sure it was always within easy reach.

The boy and the girl had stayed outside when their father had been taken into the house. They stood and studied Billy Joe, curious. Billy Joe guessed they didn't get to meet many other children this far out of town.

'Was Pa really near dead when you found him?' asked the boy, speaking for the first time.

'He was badly hurt, but I wouldn't call it near dead,' said Billy Joe. 'Andy likes to make things seem more exciting than they are.' He smiled at the two children. 'Andy's the one with the dog. That's Jess and Shane who went in with your Pa and Ma. My name's Billy Joe Ford.'

'I'm Jack,' said the boy. 'This is Manda, my sister. We're twins.'

Billy Joe studied them. They didn't look much alike, except for their carroty red hair. Jack was short and stocky, while his sister was thin and very frail looking. He noticed Manda had a slate hanging on a piece of string from the belt of her dress. It looked odd, but then there was no accounting for what people wore or how they looked, thought Billy Joe.

'Hi, Manda,' nodded Billy Joe.

The girl nodded, but didn't reply.

'She don't talk much,' said Jack. 'She's got something not right with her throat. That's why we come out West. Ma and Pa reckon the air here will be better for Manda. When she's got something to say, she writes on the slate.'

Writing on a slate, thought Billy Joe. That would only work if people could read. That wouldn't be much good for him and Jess and Andy.

Billy Joe looked at Manda. *She sure is pale*, he thought. *Pale and sickly looking.* She looked the way people look when they're going to get sick and die, but that was usually old people. He'd never seen anyone as young as this look so frail. He wondered what her illness was and if it was catching?

CHAPTER 7

William Amberson was obviously made of strong stuff. Within an hour of arriving back at the ranch, he was up and walking around, although stiffly. He had allowed his wife to wipe the blood from his face and clean his cuts, then wrap a bandage around his chest. As soon as that was done, he had insisted they all sit down at the big table in the centre of the large main room and join together for a meal.

Mrs Amberson, aided by Jack and Manda, produced bread and cheese and cuts of meat, which they set out on platters on the big wooden table. The boys gaped at the food in wonder. They hadn't eaten this well in a long time. As they tucked in, Billy Joe noticed Andy cutting off bits of meat and knew they were going to be fed to Patch later.

'It sure was lucky for me you boys was passing by,' said Mr Amberson. He was a big, jovial man with a hearty smile, which he aimed at everyone, especially at his daughter, Manda. Manda sat next to him at the table and smiled wanly back. Billy Joe noticed that she didn't eat much, and what she did put in her mouth she took a long time chewing.

'It wasn't exactly luck, Mr Amberson,' said Jess. 'We was comin' here particular to see you.'

'Oh?' said Amberson.

'Did my sister Amy send you?' asked Mrs Amberson in her city voice. 'Is anything amiss?'

'She's fine, ma'am,' nodded Jess, in between stuffing cheese and slices of cold meat into his mouth. 'No, we came out here to offer ourselves for work.'

'Work?' queried Amberson, puzzled.

'Yes, sir,' said Jess.

'We ain't got nowhere to live!' burst out Andy. 'The Mayor threw us out of our home so he can tear it down and sell the land!'

Mrs Amberson looked shocked.

'Why, that's terrible!' she said. Then she frowned. 'But I'm not sure we've got much work around here for you boys. What we're looking for is cowhands to take care of the cattle.'

Jess nodded.

'Yes, ma'am. That's us,' he said.

Again, Mrs Amberson gave a concerned frown.

'I'm not sure if you understand what we need,' she said. 'Cattle is hard work. Men's work.'

'We can look after cattle, ma'am,' said Jess. 'Me and Shane here can ride pretty well. And we've been doin' heavy work for a long time now. I work sometimes down at Schmidt's forge in Drygulch, so I know how to use a brandin' iron.'

'W-we're really g-good hard workers!' put in Shane enthusiastically.

'I'm sure,' said Mrs Amberson, 'but herding cattle –'

'We also hear you're having trouble getting men cos of the big cattle baron, Colonel McVie,' added Jess.

William Amberson laughed.

'You hear right,' he said. 'It seems Mr McVie has a way of getting what he wants round here. I wish we'd known that before we sold up and moved out here from Chicago.'

'You aren't regretting coming out here, William?' asked Mrs Amberson, a note of alarm in her voice.

Amberson shook his head.

'No, Becky. Not at all. This is what I've always wanted to do. Raise cattle and live out in good clean air.' And he smiled fondly at young Manda and Jack, who both smiled back at him. 'I thought it might be difficult, maybe with Indians and all, but I never counted on someone like McVie.' He grinned at the boys. 'I'm sure we will get some cowhands to work for us in time, but it's just gonna take a bit longer than I thought. So, in the meantime, if you boys think you can do the job –'

'We can!' said Jess firmly. 'Thank you, Mr Amberson.'
Mrs Amberson still looked unconvinced.

'I think you ought to think carefully about what you're asking these boys to do, William,' she said. 'Running cattle isn't just hard and heavy work, it's dangerous. That boy there doesn't look to be much older than Manda and Jack.' Then she pointed at Andy. 'And as for that one! Would you put your son on a horse and let him out on the open range, looking after cattle?'

'No, bu—'

'Then why would you do it with these boys?' demanded Mrs Amberson.

'Because not all boys are the same,' said Mr Amberson steadily. 'Adam Holtz is just eighteen, that's only five years older than Jess here, and he's setting up his own homestead out here.'

'But the situation here is much more dangerous than we ever reckoned, William,' insisted Mrs Amberson. 'We've already seen what McVie's men did to you today. These boys are not going to be much of a match for them.'

'You're wrong there, Becky,' said Amberson. 'These two boys,' and he gestured at Jess and Billy Joe, 'took the guns off those two and ran them off with their tails between their legs. They've got courage, for sure.' He pointed at Shane. 'I know Shane from Pedersen's livery stable in town. He's a fine boy. Honest and hard-working. Everyone says so. That's good enough recommendation for me.'

'And Andy here is a good worker, too,' said Jess. 'He can do anything you want him to do around the house or around the yard.'

'And Patch is great at catching rats,' added Andy.

Amberson looked at his wife and smiled.

'There you are, Becky. What do you say now? Are you convinced?'

Mrs Amberson shook her head.

'Then I'm afraid we must disagree, my dear,' said Amberson. 'Like I say, I've seen these boys in action, I know what they can do.' He turned to the boys. 'Gentlemen, we're glad to have you aboard.'

CHAPTER 8

After the meal, Billy Joe sat on the steps of the Amberson's porch and thought about their situation. They were going to be riding herd, looking after cattle. At the time Jess had suggested it, Billy Joe had gone along with it because the boys didn't seem to have much of a choice. Also, he didn't think the Ambersons would agree. Billy Joe thought they'd ride out, get a meal and a place to stay for a couple of nights, and – if they were lucky – land themselves work around the ranch doing odd jobs. But it looked as if he, Jess and Shane were actually going to be out on the range, on horseback, tending cattle and the thought made Billy Joe feel sick to his stomach.

He'd never been a great one for riding horses. He'd done it sometimes for sure, riding alongside his Pa. When his Pa had money, they'd buy a couple of horses. A big one for John Ford and a smaller one for Billy Joe.

But they'd usually run out of money when his Pa's gambling failed and they'd sell the horses. So mostly they'd walked, or hitched lifts from town to town on a stage or a buckboard.

Truth to tell, Billy Joe preferred riding on a buckboard or a stage. They bounced a lot and shook you up, but not as much as being on the back of a horse. And those hard saddles sure made your butt ache!

I'm gonna have to tell Jess I can't do this, thought Billy Joe. *Him and Shane can look after the cattle and the horses. I'll do other things.* But what other things? Little Andy had been given the task of doing jobs and errands around the ranch. Billy Joe was the next oldest after Jess. He'd be expected to carry his weight. And, with a sinking heart, Billy Joe knew that meant being out on the range, sitting on a horse, surrounded by thousands of dangerous-looking steers.

He was going to have to move on. But where to? And how would he live?

'Big, ain't it,' said a small voice.

He looked round. It was young Jack.

Billy Joe nodded.

'It sure is,' he said.

Jack sat down beside Billy Joe on the step. The boys looked out at the vast expanse of open range. As far as the eye could see there was just dusty ground and patches of grass, stretching out to the blue mountains in the far distance. No other human being was around for miles.

Billy Joe saw that Manda had come out of the house and was kneeling beside a patch of ground that had been dug up near the house. This patch of earth looked darker than the dusty yellow ground around it, and Manda was digging into it with a small trowel.

'What's she doin'?' asked Billy Joe. 'She buryin' somethin'?'

'She's planting vegetables,' said Jack, and now Billy Joe saw the tiny plants on the ground next to her. 'She always wanted to do it when we were in Chicago, but we didn't have anywhere to plant stuff. It was all big buildings everywhere. You ever been to Chicago?'

Billy Joe shook his head.

'It's OK,' said Jack, 'but it's crowded and noisy. Not like here.'

'You like it out here?' asked Billy Joe.

Jack hesitated, then he nodded slowly. 'I think so,' he said. 'We ain't been here that long. I like it because it's big. But at the same time it frightens me sometimes because it's so big.' He turned to Billy Joe, and his voice became hushed with concern. 'Is it true there are Indians out here and they kill people?'

'There are Indians, sure, but they ain't no more dangerous than anybody else,' said Billy Joe. 'Them men who beat your Pa up today are more dangerous than any Indians.'

'I heard Andy say to Ma that you're part-Indian,' said Jack. 'Is that so?'

Billy Joe cursed Andy for shooting his mouth off the way he did. Saying things he didn't ought to. Doing things he shouldn't.

'I guess so,' he acknowledged.

'That'll be good if the Indians ever catch you,' said Jack. 'They'll treat you good cos you're one of them.'

Billy Joe shook his head.

'I ain't an Indian to the Indians,' he said. 'To them I'm white folk.' Ruefully, he added, 'An' to lots of white folk I'm a pesky Indian. Guess I ain't no place.'

'That's tough,' said Jack.

'Not really,' said Billy Joe. 'This way I'm me, not just part of some tribe or race of people just cos of my skin. Anyway, I got my own tribe.' And he gestured towards where Mr Amberson was showing Jess and Shane around the ranch, and where Andy had just run out of the house with Patch. 'And it's the best tribe there is.'

And it is, thought Billy Joe. *So I guess I'll be staying right here.*

CHAPTER 9

The next morning, while they were all at breakfast, Mr Amberson announced his plans for the day.

'I thought me and Jess might go over and call on Adam Holtz,' he said. 'He's a good young fella, and like me he's having problems getting cowhands to work for him. We thought we might put our herds together and take turns looking after them until we get more hands. How does that suit you, Jess?'

'Sounds good, Mr Amberson,' he said.

To Shane and Billy Joe, Mr Amberson said, 'I'd appreciate it if you two boys would have a look to see if you can fix up some of building work that needs to be done. Shane knows where the hammers and nails are. But don't try lifting anything too heavy. Only do what you can.'

'W-we'll be f-fine, Mr Amberson,' said Shane. 'Me an' B-Billy Joe are str-stronger than we look.'

'Good,' beamed Mr Amberson. 'We have a plan! Things are happening!'

Once breakfast was over, and Mr Amberson and Jess had ridden off for Holtz's ranch, Billy Joe and Shane set to work on the building. The first thing they did was sort out the timber, putting the larger bits of timber in one pile and the smaller bits in another.

'That way we won't fall over ourselves when we're liftin' it,' said Billy Joe.

They were just hauling a length of heavy timber into place by one of the buildings, when they heard the sound of horses' hooves approaching. They looked up to see six men on horseback approaching.

'Mrs Amberson!' called Billy Joe. 'We got company!'

As Mrs Amberson hurried out from the house, Billy Joe hurried to the bunkhouse. He ran to his bedroll and pulled the pistol from its hiding place. Then he stuffed it down the back of his jeans, in his waistband. Out of sight, but close to hand if needed.

He hurried back out. Mrs Amberson was standing with Jack and Manda, with Shane and Andy just behind them. Andy was holding on to Patch.

The six men on horseback drew nearer. Billy Joe cocked up the brim of his hat and scanned them, wondering if they might be the men he and Jess had warned off the day before, but they were all strangers to him. One thing he knew for sure, though, they meant trouble. He could see it in their faces.

The man at the front was an older thickset man, maybe in his forties. He snapped an order, and the other five men pulled their horses to a halt and waited at a distance from the house. The older man slowed his horse down and trotted it up to the house. He was wearing a Stetson hat, which he lifted in polite greeting. With his hat off Billy Joe saw the man's hair was grey, which made him even older. Billy Joe guessed he must be at least fifty.

'Mrs Amberson, I believe,' said the man.

'You believe right,' nodded Mrs Amberson warily.

The man forced a smile, but even from a distance Billy Joe could see that it wasn't a genuine smile. The man's mouth made the shape of a smile, but his eyes stayed glittering and unfriendly.

'My name is Colonel John McVie,' he said. 'May I come in?'

McVie! The name caused Billy Joe's heart to leap, and he found his fingers reaching round behind his back and touching the handle of the gun in his waistband. This was the man who had sent the men to beat William Amberson half to death. This was the man who was scaring off anyone who might work for Amberson or Holtz.

Billy Joe looked towards the five men who sat astride their horses and watched, silently. He recognised the type. Killers, every one. One of them in particular, who was slightly at the front of the other four, looked particularly dangerous. It wasn't so much his clothes, all black from his black hat to the tips of his black boots, but the cold hard look in his eyes. Billy Joe had seen that kind of man so often in his short life. He spotted the silver Marshal's badge on the man's waistcoat. He may be wearing the badge of a lawman, but he was a hired killer, thought Billy Joe. Five hardened gunmen and McVie against Mrs Amberson and her two children, the three Drygulch boys and Patch. If it came to a gunfight they'd all be dead for sure.

Mrs Amberson looked at McVie and shook her head firmly.

'No you may not, Mr McVie' she said. 'Yesterday your men beat my husband to within an inch of his life and nearly killed him. I hear they did it on your orders. If you think I'm allowing you to enter my house, you are very much mistaken.'

McVie hesitated, then he nodded.

'I can only offer my apologies for what happened to your husband, m'am,' he said. 'It is true my men came to talk to your husband on my orders, but I did not tell them to beat him. I'm afraid that cowboys are rough men with rough ways. Obviously they misinterpreted my remarks about persuading your husband to take down his fences. I'm sorry for that.'

'No you aren't.' said Mrs Amberson. 'I know all about men like you, Colonel McVie. You're used to getting your own way, and you don't care how you do it. We had the same sort as you back in Chicago. Bullies and cowards.'

The expression on the Colonel's face tightened angrily.

'You may call me a bully, ma'am, but no one ever calls me a coward,' he said grimly.

'Then what would you call a man who comes calling at a woman's house when her husband is out, with a gang of armed ruffians to threaten her?' demanded Mrs Amberson.

'I'm not here to threaten you, ma'am,' said McVie. 'And these men aren't ruffians. They are officers of the law.'

Mrs Amberson looked at the five men and let out a harsh laugh.

'Officers of the law?' she repeated mockingly.

'At the moment Marshal Brickman and his deputies are working for me in a private capacity,' explained McVie. 'They're acting as Regulators.'

'Regulating what?'

'To stop you people stealing my cattle.'

'Why would we steal your cattle when we've got beasts of our own?' demanded Mrs Amberson.

'Then you won't mind if we take a look at your cattle and check their brands,' said McVie.

'Yes I do mind,' retorted Mrs Amberson angrily. 'You come here accusing us of being cattle thieves!

How do we know you haven't been stealing *our* cattle and putting *your* brand on them?'

McVie swallowed and Billy Joe could see the anger building up in him at this latest accusation. First Mrs Amberson had called him a coward, now she was calling him a cattle thief.

'If you want to talk about checking brands on our cattle, you come back and talk to my husband,' she snapped. 'But I guess meeting a man face to face is too much for someone like you.'

McVie glared at Mrs Amberson. Billy Joe was glad that looks couldn't kill, or Mrs Amberson would have dropped down dead by now.

Struggling to keep his temper in check, McVie said carefully in a husky voice, 'If you must know, Mrs Amberson, I didn't know your husband would be out today. It was him I came to see.'

'You expected him to be here recovering from the beating your men gave him, I expect,' retorted Mrs Amberson. 'Well, Colonel, my husband isn't like that. He doesn't lie abed and moan about things. He gets on with them. Like mending the fences your men cut.'

'Then if you would tell me where your husband can be found, I'd be happy to go and see him,' countered McVie.

Mrs Amberson gave a sarcastic laugh.

'I bet you would! You and your bunch of hired killers against one man! And you claim you ain't a coward!'

And she shook her head. Her mouth was wide in a grin, but she wasn't smiling for real.

Billy Joe could see that McVie was really struggling to control his anger, but there was no mistaking the fury in the Colonel's eyes as she mocked him. He didn't care to be humiliated in front of the gunmen he had hired.

'Mrs Amberson,' he said firmly. 'I came here today to try to clear up any misunderstanding that may have arisen . . .'

'Misunderstanding?' snapped Mrs Amberson. 'You're the one that hasn't understood things – we haven't got your darn cat—'

'But,' snapped McVie, cutting her off as he growled the word at her, 'our other situation remains the same. This is open range. There's no room for fences here. My cattle and my horses have always roamed and grazed here and I won't have that impeded. Not by your husband, not by the Government, not by a whole bunch of homesteaders.'

He leaned forward and glared darkly at her, and as he did so Billy Joe's hands automatically tightened on the butt of his pistol.

'I fought for the right to graze this land, Mrs Amberson,' continued McVie, his voice hard. 'I fought Indians and I fought rustlers to get it. My wife and two of my sons are buried out on this land. So are many of my friends who worked with me. They gave their lives so we could open this range. I ain't gonna let you and your husband and his like shut it now, not after what we gave for it. Please pass that message on to your husband.' With that he touched the brim of his hat and he nodded unsmiling at her. 'I'll wish you good-day, ma'am.'

He headed towards his horse. As he was about to mount it, he stopped and turned towards the Shane and Billy Joe.

'I understand that two of you boys aimed guns at my men yesterday and threatened to shoot them,' he said grimly. 'That was brave, and I admire bravery. But be under no mistake: if anyone draws a gun on me or mine again, I'll have them shot down like dogs. Boys or not.'

With that, McVie gestured at the other men, and they turned their horses and rode off.

Billy Joe released his fingers from the handle of his gun, and let out a long heartfelt sigh of relief.

CHAPTER 10

Jess and Amberson rode alongside one another, their horses trotting close to the wire fence that kept Amberson's cattle away from McVie's on the open range.

'This way we can check the fence as we ride over to Adam's place,' said Mr Amberson. 'I don't trust McVie not to send his men out to pull it down.'

So far the fence had been intact and the cattle grazing contentedly on both sides of it.

'I think you'll like Adam,' said Amberson. 'Like I say, he's young. Just eighteen. And he's not long married. He came out first to get the house ready for his wife, Dorcas. She's coming out to join him next month.' He smiled. 'Adam and Dorcas and us are the first of a whole new breed of cattle ranchers. Adam's from Boston and we're from Chicago. We bought the land from a Government Agent back

East. I tell you, Jess, it won't be long before this whole range is full of small ranches like ours.'

'I can't see Colonel McVie liking that,' said Jess.

Amberson chuckled.

'It's Government policy,' he said shrugging. 'The Colonel is gonna have to live with it, whether he likes it or not.'

'It don't look like he feels that way,' said Jess, doubtfully. 'Not from the way his men was kickin' you yesterday.'

'He'll fall into line,' said Amberson. 'It'll take a bit of time, but he will. It's the Law. Ain't no man bigger than the Law.'

'That may be so back east in places like Chicago and Boston, but out here in the west thing are different,' said Jess. 'To be honest, Mr Amberson, the Law sometimes applies in the towns here in the west, but out on the open range there ain't no law as such. It's just too big for even a heap of Marshals to look after it.

Amberson shook his head.

'I hear what you say, Jess, but the Government won't let it stay that way. Trust me.'

'The Government ain't out here, Mr Amberson,' commented Jess. 'The truth is, ain't nothin' out here but cattle, men with guns, and Indians, and they either get along together or they don't. People here tend to make their own law.'

Again, Amberson shook his head.

'That's the old way, Jess,' he said. 'Those bad old days are behind us now. Law and Order is comin' to this land. Civilisation. Ain't nothin' can stop it. That's progress.'

Jess fell silent and carried on riding. He admired Mr Amberson's overflowing confidence and optimism, but it couldn't outweigh his sense of foreboding. Amberson had already received one bad beating from McVie's men. The next time it could be a lot worse.

* * *

'Welcome!'

Adam Holtz may have been only five years older than Jess, but he looked a lot older. Adam was tall, broad and muscular. He had also grown a moustache to try and make him look even more grown-up. It didn't really work, but Jess admired Adam for trying.

Jess and Amberson got down from their horses and shook hands with Adam. Jess looked around the land. The ranch house was barely begun, just piles of ready-split logs stacked. The 'housing' was two large tents made from oiled canvas stretched over wooden structures.

'This here's Jess,' Amberson said, introducing the two. 'Him and a bunch of boys have come to work for me, herding cattle.'

'Howdy,' smiled Adam, and Jess shook his hand. It was a good firm handshake. Jess smiled back, liking Adam Holtz straightaway.

'Pleased to meet you, Mr Holtz,' said Jess.

'Call me Adam,' said Holtz. He looked at Jess doubtfully. 'Aren't you a little young to be herding cattle?'

'Me and my pals can do most any thing a bigger man can do,' said Jess confidently.

Adam smiled broadly.

'That's good to hear,' he said. 'We can do with some good help to get us established.'

Amberson shot a look at the two tents, their sides flapping slightly in the breeze.

'I see you ain't managed to get on with the house yet, Adam.'

'Too many things to do, William,' replied Adam. 'As I see it, the priority was to get the land fenced and the cattle grazing. It's the cattle that are going be the money for us, and they need to be fattened up nicely.'

'Does Dorcas know what she's coming to?' asked Amberson.

Adam gave a rueful smile.

'She thinks she's coming out to a proper ranch house,' he admitted. 'But I'm sure she won't mind living in a tent for a week or two. The main thing is we're going to be together.' To Jess, he added, 'We've only been married six months, and for the last four of those I've been out here on Blue Ridge getting this place ready.'

Not getting it ready fast enough, thought Jess. He wondered what Adam's wife would say when she realised she would be living in a draughty tent.

Adam must have seen the doubtful look on Jess's face, because he said: 'There's been a whole heap to do out here. There was twenty miles of fencing to put up, and it's hard work for a man on his own.' His face darkened. 'Now some of that fence has come down, and a few of my cattle gone.'

'McVie?' asked Amberson.

'Maybe,' shrugged Adam. 'Maybe it's Indians. Could be rustlers. Or maybe it was just an accident and the cattle broke through the fence and strayed.'

'How many cattle you lost?' asked Amberson.

'About thirty head,' said Adam. 'That's a lot of money gone missing.' He sighed. 'So I've spent a lot of time in the saddle lately, riding the fence-line and making sure I don't lose any more.' He hesitated, and then asked awkwardly, 'To be honest, it sure would be a help if your young man here could give me a hand for a while. With Dorcas coming out in the next two weeks, I'm finding it pretty hard managing on my own.'

Mr Amberson frowned.

'We got a lot of work on ourselves, Adam,' he began doubtfully. When he saw the young rancher's face fall, he immediately changed tack. He forced a broad smile and finished, 'but, if Jess don't mind, I'm sure we could spare him for a day.'

Adam's face lit up.

'Are you sure, William?' he asked eagerly.

'That's what neighbours are for,' smiled Amberson. 'But it ain't up to me. It's up to Jess here. He's the one who'll be doing the work.'

Adam looked at Jess keenly.

'I sure would appreciate it, Jess,' he said. 'It would make an awful difference to me.'

Jess grinned. This would be something new and exciting, helping to get a whole new ranch started up from scratch. It was the stuff of the pioneers.

'I'd be very pleased to.' said Jess. 'What work you got in mind?'

'A day checking the fence with me,' said Adam. 'I've got tools, and if we find it broken we can fix it. Also rounding up any strays.'

Jess nodded. Travelling the open range, and carving out the land for people to live here. That was something he wanted to do – he felt it right through to his bones.

'If Mr Amberson says it's OK by him, then it's OK by me,' he said looking over at Amberson.

'Great!' said Adam delightedly, then he gave them both an apologetic smile. 'Here am I asking a big favour, and I haven't even given you coffee or something to chew on!' he said. 'At the moment I've only got biscuits, but all that'll change once Dorcas gets here.'

'Biscuits will be just fine, Adam,' said Amberson cheerfully.

Adam bustled around, producing a blackened coffee pot and he set coffee to brew on a small open fire, while he opened up a tin of biscuits and passed them around. Jess was hungry, but he was careful to only take two biscuits. He guessed that the young rancher was short of food, as well as money.

The three sat around the fire talking, though mainly it was Amberson and Adam Holtz who did the talking. Jess listened to the plans the men had for Blue Ridge, for their ranches, for a whole new way of life out here in the West. Both men seemed to see a day when this area was covered by a string of ranches, all joined up and working together, supplying the big cities back east with meat and bringing money and prosperity to Drygulch.

Jess drank his coffee and sat and listened, and thought how strange it was. Both men were from back East, and they were planning to bring Eastern ways out to the West – business and order and organisation. It was a different way of life from what Jess had known. In the West, things just happened. Sometimes good, sometimes bad. Fencing this huge country and trying to organise it was the eastern way of doing things. Jess wondered how long it would be before east and west clashed face to face out here, and things turned really bad.

CHAPTER 11

Mr Amberson headed home late in the afternoon, leaving Jess and Adam on their own. Adam prepared a meal of salted dried meat with bread, which Jess admitted tasted pretty good, then they bunked down for the night inside the biggest tent.

Next morning, they were both up early and, after coffee, Jess followed Adam into the tent to collect up the tools they'd need for fixing any broken sections of fence. Adam noticed the way Jess limped, and asked, 'What happened to your leg, Jess, if you don't mind my asking?'

'I got shot,' said Jess simply.

'Who by?'

'A gunman,' replied Jess. 'He and his gang were trying to hold up the bank in Drygulch.' His face darkened at the painful memory. 'I lost a good friend in the same trouble. They shot him dead.'

Adam shook his head sadly.

'Guns, Jess,' he said. 'They're to blame, that's what Dorcas says. She says we shouldn't carry weapons of any kind. It's her religion.'

'What religion's that?' asked Jess.

'They're called Quakers,' said Adam. 'She told me I had to be a Quaker too when I married her, so I guess I am as well.'

'What's bein' a Quaker mean?' asked Jess.

Adam shrugged.

'I ain't found out yet cos of me and Dorcas not spending much time together so far,' he admitted. 'But Dorcas will teach me properly when she gets here. The main thing is you've gotta be peaceful. That's what Dorcas says.'

'Maybe,' agreed Jess, he wanted to believe that. 'Though some folks say a gun isn't so bad in the right hands. It's when it's in the wrong hands you get folks killed.'

'That's not what Dorcas says. She says all killing is wrong.'

'What about killin' for self-defence?' asked Jess.

Adam shook his head again.

'Dorcas says any sort of killing is wrong,' he said again.

'So if she was bein' attacked by cowboys with guns, or Indians, you wouldn't do nothin' to save her?' asked Jess, curious.

Adam gave a big sigh.

'Truth to tell, Jess, despite what Dorcas says, I think I would. I guess I'm not as strong in my faith as Dorcas. Which is why I don't carry a gun, so I can't give into temptation.' He looked at Jess. 'I guess you think I must be weak to do that, Jess?'

It was Jess's turn to shake his head.

'No, Adam, I don't think you're weak at all,' he said. 'Me, I don't carry a gun neither. Seems to me if you carry a gun, sooner or later you're gonna be tempted to use it. Or someone is gonna be tempted to see how good you are with it, which ends up as the same thing.'

They carried the tools outside and Jess began to bundle them up, ready to put on the horses, while Adam went back into the tent to pack provisions for their journey. As Jess tied the tools up, he spotted eight horsemen approaching. From the dust kicking up behind them, they were travelling fast.

'Looks like we got visitors, Adam!' he called.

Adam hurried out of the tent and stood by Jess. As he saw the men in the distance his expression turned grim.

'I guess it's McVie's men!' he said.

'They been here before?' asked Jess.

Adam shook his head.

'No,' he said. 'But a couple of weeks ago I had a visit from McVie himself, suggesting I get off this land. I guess the fact I'm still here means he's decided to send some of his men to strong-arm me.' His face set firm. 'But I'm not going anywhere.'

Jess remembered the sight of two of McVie's men kicking William Amberson, and his heart sank. These were eight men.

'Maybe this would be a good time to have a gun, Adam,' murmured Jess, thinking of the rifle he'd left back at the Ambersons' ranch. He might not like guns himself, but he knew what effect a gun could have when there was trouble brewing. Like now. Although one rifle wouldn't have been much good against eight armed men. And they were armed, he was sure of that.

The horsemen arrived by the tents and Jess was disturbed to see that two of them were the men he and Billy Joe had chased off the other day: Mack and Sandy. Both men recognised him, because Jess saw the two exchange triumphant smiles.

'Well, well, looka here!' smirked Mack. 'It's that kid who run us off!' He gave Jess a nasty grin. 'I sure am pleased to be meeting you again, kid! I think you got something of mine . . .'

Jess saw the man glance down at Jess's waist, looking for his gun. The boy tensed, wondering what Mack was going to do? He had another gun in his holster. Was he going to draw it? The man at the front turned to Mack.

'That's enough of that,!' he said. 'One thing at a time. Let's do what we came here to do first.'

'But he took our guns off us the other day, Brick!' complained Mack. 'Mine and Sandy's!'

'Yeah!' added Sandy. 'That gun's my property! I want it back!'

'I said that's enough!' commanded the man called Brick.

Jess turned his attention to him. He was obviously the leader of the bunch. He wore black trousers, and a black waistcoat over his shirt. His hat was black too. He looked like an undertaker on a horse. The two things that said he wasn't an undertaker were the six-guns in the holsters at his sides, and the Marshal's badge on his waistcoat.

So he was a Marshal. Which meant the five men with him were either his posse or his deputies. Amberson and Adam had said they wanted the Law. Well, this man in black was it.

The expression on the man's face was grim and hard. Jess had seen that same look on so many men's faces. It was a killer's face; hard, cold, unemotional. Not exactly what Jess's friends had wanted.

The man sat astride his horse and looked down at Adam, and asked, 'Your name Holtz?'

'What if it is?' demanded Adam.

'My name's Brickman,' said the tall man. 'Marshal Brickman. Me and my men here are employed by Colonel McVie to stop people like you rustlin' his cattle.'

'I haven't rustled anybody's cattle!' retorted Adam angrily.

'No?' said Brickman. 'Well we just been doin' some checkin' on some of your steers we found on the way here, and they sure got some unusual brandin' on 'em. It looks to me like it was Colonel McVie's brand been covered over with another brand. Yours, by the look of it.'

'That's nonsense!' said Adam. He looked wildly from Brickman to the other men. 'I've never branded any other cattle but my own!'

'Well it don't look that way to me,' said Brickman. 'But I'm sure we can clear this up, if you come with us.'

Adam looked bewildered.

'Come with you?' he demanded. 'Where? Why?'

'We're taking you to Drygulch on a charge of cattle rustlin',' said Brickman. 'You'll stay in jail there till the County Marshal comes and arrests you, then you'll stand trial, and we'll hang you.'

'Why don't we just hang him now and save all that trouble,' chuckled one of the men.

Jess found himself hardly able to breathe. Eight killers against the two of them, and neither he nor Adam Holtz were armed.

'I'm not going anywhere with you!' said Adam angrily. 'You think I don't know what this is? You're just a lynching party!'

'Wrong, mister,' snapped Brickman. 'We're law

officers authorised to maintain the law in this territory. So get your hat and come with us.'

Adam shook his head and stared defiantly at Brickman.

'No,' he said. 'I haven't ever stolen and re-branded cattle. And there's a way to prove this. Let's go see those cattle.'

Brickman scowled.

'You callin' me a liar!' he demanded.

'Take it whichever way you want,' snapped Adam. 'If there's any re-branding being done, it isn't by me. And I'll prove it!'

'Is that so?' growled Brickman. The Marshal's face hardened and his eyes narrowed almost into slits. Like a snake's eyes just before it strikes, thought Jess.

And then, before Jess knew what was happening, Brickman pulled his gun from its holster and shot Adam twice. Adam gaped, put his hand to his chest as the blood poured out, soaking his shirt, then collapsed on the ground in a crumpled heap.

CHAPTER 12

Jess stared at Adam's dead body, shocked to the core. Then he whirled round to face Brickman. Brickman trained his gun on Jess.

'Don't try anything foolish, boy!' said Brickman. 'You already seen I ain't afraid to use this thing.'

'You killed him!' said the stunned Jess. 'You murdered him!'

Brickman shook his head.

'It weren't murder, it was self defence,' he said. 'He was reaching for his back pocket. He was going for a gun to shoot me.'

'He didn't even have a gunbelt on!' said Jess. 'Look!'

'Well, he was going for a knife, then,' said Brickman. 'Ain't no way I'm gonna give anyone the chance to get first drop on me.'

'He didn't have a knife!' raged Jess. 'You gunned down an unarmed man! That makes you a murderer!'

Brickman's face tensed.

'I'd watch that mouth of yours, boy,' he warned. 'Accusations like that can get someone killed. Maybe you'd like to try your luck and pull a gun on me.'

'I don't have a gun,' said Jess, then he added pointedly, 'But then, that didn't stop you killing Adam.'

'I think you're mistaken,' said Brickman. 'My men clearly saw young Holtz here going for his back pocket. Ain't that right, boys?'

'Sure is,' said the man called Mack, and the others joined in with nods and grunts of agreement.

'So better remember that before you start spreadin' lies about what happened here,' said Brickman to Jess. Turning to his men, he said, 'All righty, boys. Guess we've done what we came to do. Time to move on.'

'You won't get away with this!' shouted Jess. The sense of injustice at what had just happened filled him with anger. 'I'm gonna make sure the Law finds out and you hang for this!'

'I am the Law,' snapped Brickman. And with that he fired three shots near Jess's feet, each one making Jess leap back as the dirt spurted up around him.

'Any one of those bullets coulda killed you, boy!' spat Brickman. 'Next time one of 'em will.'

With that, Brickman yanked his horse round and spurred it on, the rest of the men following. All except Mack and Sandy, who hung back and looked down at Jess with smug satisfaction.

'I told you we'd meet again,' said Sandy menacingly. He tapped the gun in his holster. 'If you like, you can say all those things you said to us before, and let's see what happens.'

Jess could tell these men wanted to shoot him. But he wasn't going to give them the satisfaction of letting them see he was scared, even though his heart was thumping fit to burst and his throat was dry tight with fear. Their horses edged closer.

'And we still want our guns back!' snarled Mack. 'Next time we see you, you'd better have 'em for us.'

'Mack! Sandy! Leave him be and come on!' called Brickman.

The two cowboys hesitated, then Mack spat on the ground by Jess's feet. They turned their horses and rode after their companions.

Jess hurried to Adam and knelt down beside him. His friend was dead, his eyes wide open and staring. There was no pulse, nothing but a pool of blood staining the dusty ground. All of Adam and Dorcas Holtz's dreams were gone with those two bullets.

CHAPTER 13

At the Amberson ranch, Billy Joe was helping Mr Amberson carry timber for the new building. Andy was helping Mrs Amberson and Jack in the house. Shane had been tending the horses in the stable, something he was good at and liked doing. Horses didn't mind him stuttering. He left the stable and saw Manda by the small plot of earth in which she was growing her plants. She was putting a row of stones along the edge of the bed to mark it out. Shane walked over and joined her.

'St-stones ain't always the b-best th-thing for th-that,' he said. 'S-sometimes s-s-snakes 'n things get under 'em cos it's c-cool for 'em. You g-g-gotta watch out for s-snakes.'

Manda looked up at Shane, and smiled and nodded. But she still carried on putting the stones in a line at the edge of the bed. Shane hesitated, then he crouched down beside her. He gestured at the slate hanging from Manda's belt. 'If you w-wanna talk to me, I can read,' he said. 'Not big words, but most.'

Manda looked at him, studying his face.

'I-it must be d-difficult n-not talkin',' added Shane. 'It's h-hard for me as it is cos I g-got this st-st-stammer.'

Manda hesitated, as if wondering what to do next. Then she pulled a piece of chalk from the pocket of her dress and wrote on the slate. 'How old are you?'

'I'm n-nine,' said Shane.

Manda gave him a smile. *She was testing me*, thought Shane, *seeing if I could really read*.

'H-have you always b-been l-l-like this?' asked Shane. 'Not bein' able to t-talk?'

Manda shook her head. She rubbed out the chalk words on her slate, and replaced them by writing: 'It began a year ago.'

'I b-bin t-talkin' like th-this s-since I w-was l-little,' said Shane. 'I d-don't know w-why. My br-brother P-P-Pete said it was c-cos of wh-what happened wh-when we was small.' He saw her puzzled look and smiled sadly. 'P-Pete got sh-shot a coupla m-months ago.' The smile vanished, and his eyes lowered. 'I m-miss him a l-lot.'

As he said the words, Shane felt tears welling up inside him. It happened now and then. He guessed it always would. He felt a gentle touch on his cheek, and he looked up to see Manda looking at him, her fingers touching his face, a look of concern. He forced another smile, an apologetic one.

'I-I'm s-sorry . . .' he began.

The sound of hurrying hooves thundering on the ground came to their ears, and both he and Manda looked up in alarm. They recognised Jess's horse heading towards the ranch, dust flying up behind it as it raced at speed towards them. Before they knew it, Jess had pulled the horse to a halt and leapt out of the saddle.

The Ambersons, and Billy Joe and Andy, had all hurried out at hearing the fast-approaching hoofbeats.

'It's Adam Holtz!' called Jess urgently. 'He's been shot! He's dead!'

Mr and Mrs Amberson exchanged looks of horror, and the children clustered around Jess, plying him with questions.

'Who did it?' demanded Billy Joe.

'H-how?' asked Shane, shocked. 'W-w-why?'

Mr Amberson strode forward.

'Tell us exactly what happened,' he demanded grimly.

As quickly as he could, Jess told them the events at Holtz's ranch: Marshal Brickman and his men arriving; the accusation of cattle stealing; the way Adam was shot.

When Jess had finished, Mr Amberson's normally cheerful expression was grim and serious.

'This is murder,' he said.

'Yes,' agreed Jess. 'Plain and simple.'

'So why didn't he shoot you as well, Jess?' asked Billy Joe, puzzled. 'You was a witness.'

Jess shook his head.

'I don't know,' he admitted. 'I been thinkin' about that all the way here.'

'I think I can guess why,' said Amberson quietly. 'He left Jess alive because he wants everyone to know who shot Adam dead and why. He knew Jess would come and tell us. This way he hopes the word will spread that anyone who interferes with McVie's plans will end up dead. He wants to scare us off, and stop other homesteaders from coming here.'

'Where is Adam now?' asked Mrs Amberson.

'I buried him best I could,' said Jess. 'I dug a shallow grave and put dirt and rocks on him, to stop the coyotes and vultures gettin' to him.'

'We'll give him a proper burial later,' said Amberson. 'Right now we have to get the people responsible for this!'

'You're not goin' after them, William?' asked Mrs Amberson, shocked. 'They'll kill you!'

'No,' said Amberson. 'I'm going into town and reporting this to the Sheriff.'

'The man who shot Adam wore a badge,' Jess informed him. 'He said he was a Marshal.'

'A man dressed all in black?' asked Mrs Amberson. Jess nodded.

'He was here with McVie yesterday,' Mrs Amberson told her husband. 'McVie said he was a Marshal working for him.'

'That's nonsense!' snorted Amberson. 'These men are just cold-hearted killers! What they have done is against the law, and I'll see they hang for it!'

'Say they come here next, Pa?' asked Jack nervously. 'What do we do?'

Amberson fell silent and he looked at Jack and Manda, looking up at him.

'We'll go into town,' said Jess.

Amberson glanced sharply at Jess.

'You need to be here to protect your family, Mr Amberson,' said Jess. 'We know the Sheriff. We'll go into town and tell him what happened.'

'Andy and P-Patch better st-stay here,' said Shane. 'So one of us ha-had b-better stay here with them, in c-case anything ha-happens.'

'I'll go with Jess,' said Billy Joe.

Even as he said the words, Billy Joe felt a sense of surprise. He didn't like riding horses, yet here he was volunteering to ride all the way into town. But he knew the reason. He didn't want to stay here, doing nothing, being helpless, waiting for McVie or his men to turn up again. By going into town he'd be doing something.

'You can take Harvey,' spoke up Jack.

'We gave Harvey to Jack as a present when we came out here,' said Amberson. 'Jack's still too small to ride him properly –'

'No I'm not, Pa!' protested Jack. 'I'm getting bigger all the time. I ride him already, and soon I'll be able to ride him properly all the time!'

'Of course you will, son,' nodded Amberson, patting his son affectionately on the head. Turning to Billy Joe, he added, 'Harvey is a good, gentle horse. And he's fast when you want him to be. You'll be OK on him.'

'I'll go and saddle him up,' offered Jack.

'I'll h-help you,' offered Shane.

The two boys ran off to the stable to get Harvey ready.

'You gonna take your gun, Billy Joe?' asked Andy.

'I'd be a fool not to,' said Billy Joe.

'I don't think that's a good idea,' said Jess. 'If it came to a face-to-face gunfight, we couldn't beat Brickman and his men.'

'Who said anythin' about face-to-face?' demanded Billy Joe.

'This arguin' is wastin' precious time,' said

Amberson. 'Jess, let Billy Joe take his gun.'

'All right,' said Jess. Turning to Billy Joe he said, 'Come on, Billy Joe. Let's go get Harvey and ride!'

CHAPTER 14

By the time the two boys reached Drygulch, Billy Joe's bottom and legs were aching. Even though Harvey was every bit as good a horse as the Ambersons said, the saddle was hard, and Billy Joe felt like someone had been kicking him in the butt for the last two hours.

They pulled up their horses outside the Sheriff's office and hitched them to the rail. The boys were just about to step up onto the boardwalk, when a sneering voice said: 'Well well, looks like we keep bumping into you, boy!'

Jess and Billy Joe looked up sharply. Mack and Sandy, were standing on the boardwalk in front of the Sheriff's office, obviously having just come out. Behind them stood Brickman.

Sandy smiled broadly and patted his pistol.

'Got yourself a gun now, kid?' he chuckled at Jess.

He looked at Billy Joe. 'Maybe your friend has got his pistol with him again?'

Billy Joe looked at the roll of cloth with his precious pistol inside it tied to his saddle, and cursed silently. There was no way he'd have time to grab it before these men fired.

'That's enough, boys,' snapped Brickman. 'Let's move.'

'But these two boys think they're tough,' complained Mack. 'Like I told you, they took our guns off us the other day. We want 'em back!' He looked hard at Billy Joe and Jess. 'That's our property you took. That's thievin'. And thieves round here get hanged.'

'I said that's enough!' said Brickman firmly. 'If you two were fools enough to let a couple of kids take your guns, you deserve to lose 'em! And I just spent time sayin' what law-abidin' citizens we are, so let's move.' He looked coldly at Jess and Billy Joe and said quietly, 'We'll deal with these two later. Outa town.'

The menacing smiles vanished from the two men's faces, to be replaced by scowls. Sandy spat into the dirt.

'You ain't seen the last of us, boys,' he said. 'And next time you won't get saved so easy.'

With that the three gunmen walked off, heading for the saloon.

Billy Joe looked at Jess and let out a long sigh of relief.

'I thought we was dead for sure,' he said.

Jess shook his head.

'They weren't gonna shoot us down in front of the Sheriff's office,' he said.

'Sandy and Mack were goin' to,' said Billy Joe.

'That's cos they're stupid,' said Jess. 'Brickman's the real dangerous one cos he's got brains.'

'Think they'll try and ambush us out of town when we head back to the Ambersons'?' asked Billy Joe.

'Maybe,' shrugged Jess. He looked across at the Golden Dollar saloon, where the three gunmen had gone. He saw their horses tethered to the rail outside, recognising them from earlier at Adam's tent. 'That depends on whether we get our business with the Sheriff finished fast an' we can get on the road back before they leave town.'

Billy Joe looked doubtful.

'My butt sure would appreciate a rest before we head back, Jess,' he said. 'All that bouncin' and bangin' in the saddle, I don't reckon I'll be able to sit down for a week.'

'That's cos you ride against the horse instead of with it,' said Jess.

'That may be,' said Billy Joe. He sighed. 'Guess I'm gonna have to learn to ride proper.'

Billy Joe turned to Harvey, took the roll of cloth off his saddle, removed the pistol from it, and stuck it in his waistband.

'Why you doin' that?' demanded Jess.

Billy Joe gestured towards the saloon.

'I ain't leavin' it for them to take,' he replied.

Jess regarded Billy Joe with a serious look.

'Billy Joe, we need to talk about that gun of yours,' he said.

'It's kept me alive so far,' said Billy Joe defensively. Then he added, 'Maybe if Adam Holtz had had a gun on him, he'd be alive right now.'

'Not against eight gunmen,' countered Jess. 'And it ain't what happened to Adam that worries me so much as Andy.'

'Andy?' echoed Billy Joe in surprise. 'What's he got to do with it?'

'He looks up to you,' said Jess. 'If he thinks you carryin' a gun is good, pretty soon he'll think it's OK for him, too.'

'Andy's just a kid!' responded Billy Joe. 'He ain't gonna start carryin' a gun any time soon!'

'Why not?' demanded Jess. 'You gonna tell him not to, Billy Joe?'

'Sure I am!' nodded Billy Joe.

'And what are you gonna say when he says you carry one? And he saw you kill a man with it.'

'He never saw me kill him!'

'He thinks he did,' countered Jess. 'He thinks it was a great thing you shootin' that outlaw. You're his hero cos you did that!'

'I saved a town!' retorted Billy Joe, annoyed.

'Lots of people saved the town that day,' countered Jess.

Billy Joe scowled.

'I ain't havin' this conversation no more, Jess!'

'Let's hope we don't start havin' it again over Andy's dead body,' said Jess shortly. He headed towards the door of the Sheriff's office. Billy Joe scowled and followed him. He wasn't going to give up his gun, whatever Jess said.

CHAPTER 15

Inside the office, the large, round figure of Matt Stevens, Sheriff Nolan's deputy, sat behind the sheriff's desk. He grinned broadly in welcome as the two boys came in.

'Jess and Billy Joe! Well, this is a pleasure! I heard you boys were out working at the Ambersons' place.'

'Yes, sir. We are,' nodded Jess. 'But we've come into see Sheriff Nolan about something real urgent.'

The big man's smile faded and he shook his head with a sigh.

'I'm sorry, boys, but the Sheriff's not here right now.'

'Where is he?' asked Billy Joe. 'We can go find him.'

'I'm afraid he ain't even in town,' said Stevens. 'He had to go over to River Creek. He won't be back till tomorrow morning at the earliest.' Then his friendly grin reappeared. 'But he's left me in charge. You can tell me anything and I'll see what I can do about it.'

Billy Joe and Jess exchanged doubtful looks. Matt Stevens was a good man, well-meaning, but useless as a peace officer. He did his best to avoid trouble at all costs.

Billy Joe could never understand why Sheriff Nolan hired him as his deputy. Jess had told Billy Joe that Nolan preferred to have Matt Stevens around because some of the younger men were too keen to make a reputation for themselves with a gun. They shot first and asked questions afterwards. Matt Stevens would never draw a gun on anyone unless it was absolutely necessary. And right now, whatever Billy Joe thought of him, Matt Stevens was the only law officer around. After the long ride they'd had they couldn't just return to the Ambersons' without having said anything.

'I'm afraid we've come to report a murder, Mr Stevens,' said Jess.

The big man stopped smiling and looked at them in shock.

'A m-murder?' he echoed, stunned.

Jess nodded.

'Those men who were in here just now . . .'

'You mean Marshal Brickman and his deputies?' said Stevens.

Billy Joe snorted.

'Deputies! Huh!' he said sarcastically.

'They shot one of the homesteaders, Adam Holtz,' Jess said, giving Billy Joe a kick in the ankle to shut him up.

Stevens looked back at the boys, a look of bewilderment on his face.

'Jess, I don't think you've got this right . . .' he began.

'Yes I have,' said Jess firmly.

Stevens shook his head slowly.

'Marshal Brickman was in here to report the shooting,' he said, adding, 'Not that he needed to. He knows anything outside of town ain't our territory. He says he came in to report it out of courtesy, just in case wrong rumours spread. He said he shot him in self-defence. He said he went to arrest this man for rustling cattle and he went for his gun.'

'But it wasn't self defence, Mr Stevens!' said Jess angrily. 'It was murder, for sure! Brickman shot Adam Holtz right in front of my eyes. Adam didn't have no gun nor a knife nor nothin' on him!'

Rubbing his hand over his eyes, Stevens sighed.

'That ain't the story Brickman tells, Jess. And he's got his witnesses who tell the same story. And all of them are badge-wearin' lawmen.'

'Lawmen!' spat Jess. 'They're hired killers!'

'If Jess says Holtz was unarmed, then he was unarmed,' said Billy Joe angrily. 'You know Jess don't lie, Mr Stevens! And so does the Sheriff!'

Stevens nodded.

'I hear what you say, Billy Joe, and I believe *you* believe what you say, Jess, but no judge or jury will take your word against theirs. And if you try, a good lawyer will mess you up in court and make everyone think black is white and white is black.'

'But –' Billy Joe started.

'Like I said, the Sheriff's office ain't got no jurisdiction outside of Drygulch. This killin' happened out on the range, so it comes under the local Marshal.'

'And Brickman's the Marshal,' snapped Jess, angry.

The deputy shrugged.

'So Brickman gets away with it?' asked Billy Joe bitterly.

'Be fair, boys,' appealed Stevens. 'This ain't that straightforward.'

'Yes it is,' insisted Jess. 'That man murdered Adam Holtz.'

Again, Stevens shook his head.

'I wouldn't go around saying that sort of thing, Jess. You can get yourself in a heap of trouble.'

'You mean Brickman and his men might shoot me too?'

'No,' said Stevens. 'I mean they might get offended and you could find yourself in jail for making false accusations against an officer of the law.'

'This was a waste of time,' snapped Billy Joe in disgust. 'You got a killer out there and you won't do nothin' about it.'

'I can't, Billy Joe,' defended Stevens. 'Like I say, he's got witnesses. And it ain't even in the town's jurisdiction.'

'Maybe the Colonel's stealin' his own cattle so he can blame it on the homesteaders,' snapped Billy Joe. 'That'd give him the excuse to kill people like Adam Holz and frighten off the others.'

Stevens leaned forward, frowning, looking from Jess to Billy Joe and then back again.

'I've known the Colonel for years, and I can tell you he's no crook,' he said firmly. 'When he fought in the army he was a hero. Tough but fair, is what people say about him.'

'Then why does he hire killers like Brickman and his men?' demanded Jess.

'Jess, I'm giving you some serious advice here,' said Stevens warningly. 'You start making accusations against Colonel McVie, you really will be in serious trouble. He's a man who knows a lot of very powerful people.'

'And us and the Ambersons don't know anyone powerful, is that right, Mr Stevens?' demanded Jess bitterly. 'So we can all just get killed and no one will do anything about it.'

'That's not what I'm saying at all, Jess, and you know it,' said Stevens, now definitely getting angry. 'You're putting words in my mouth I never said.' He shrugged. 'But I'll leave a note for the Sheriff for when he comes back and I'm pretty sure he'll come out to the Ambersons and see you.'

'If we ain't already been shot dead,' snapped Billy Joe angrily.

Stevens didn't answer at first, just scowled. Then he said coldly: 'If you boys will excuse me, I got work to do.'

Jess's expression became grim.

'Thank you for your time, Mr Stevens. I'm sorry we wasted it.'

With that Jess turned and headed for the door.

'Come on, Billy, Joe,' he said. 'Guess we ain't gonna get any help here.'

CHAPTER 16

'That was a waste of time,' snorted Billy Joe.

Jess nodded in angry agreement.

The two boys looked along the street towards the Golden Dollar saloon. The horses of Brickman and his two gunmen were still tied to the rail outside the saloon.

'What else we gonna do now we're in town?' asked Billy Joe. 'Think we ought to go and see the Johnsons and tell 'em, what's happenin' out at Mrs Johnson's sister's?'

Jess shook his head.

'The Johnsons can't do anythin',' he said. 'And there ain't no sense in worryin' them unnecessary, like.'

Billy Joe shrugged.

'We could always go and see how our old shack is?' he suggested.

Again, Jess shook his head, and he gave a shudder.

'My guess is Mayor Redding will have torn it down by now,' he said. 'It ain't gonna give me no pleasure to go and see our home all torn down.' He looked grim. 'No, Billy Joe, we ain't got time for stuff like that. The situation's urgent. We gotta get movin'.'

'But my butt's still sore,' complained Billy Joe.

'Which would you prefer: a sore butt or a bullet in the head at an ambush?' asked Jess tensely.

'You think they'll try and kill us?' asked Billy Joe.

'They killed Adam Holz,' said Jess. 'And they know we ain't come to town and callin' on the Sheriff just to say hello. Brickman will want to shut us up. And he won't do it in town. Too many witnesses.'

Billy Joe sighed.

'So, we head back to the Ambersons?' he groaned.

Jess shook his head.

'No,' he said. 'I got me a different idea . . .'

Jess's idea was to talk directly to McVie. 'If he really is honest and straight like Deputy Stevens said, maybe he'll call off Brickman. At least, until the Sheriff gets back.'

Billy Joe was doubtful, but in the situation they were in, he guessed it was the only chance they might have.

The journey out to McVie's ranch was agony for Billy Joe. Every jolt, every bump, he felt the hard leather of the saddle crash into his backside and chafe against his legs. He'd pushed his pistol back inside the roll of cloth tied to his saddle so it didn't fall out as he rode.

Luckily, Harvey was a good horse and Billy Joe felt confident riding him. He didn't feel that Harvey was going to go crazy, or go off in a way that Billy Joe couldn't control, like some horses. But he still ached. *I ain't gonna be able to walk for a week after this*, he moaned to himself.

The two boys rode hard, eating up the miles on the road out to McVie's spread.

McVie's sprawling ranch house was set in a valley overlooked by the Blue Ridge, about ten miles from town. As with the rest of the range, McVie's cattle ranged and grazed throughout the valley.

I sure hope us riding this fast don't spook them, thought Billy Joe, *or they'll stampede and we'll be gored for sure*. Suddenly, some instinct made him take a look over his shoulder, and his heart gave a leap as he saw three riders following them, riding hard. It was Brickman, Mack and Sandy!

'Jess!' he shouted. 'Brickman and his men are hot on our tail!'

Jess threw a look over his shoulder. The expression on his face said it all: they were in deep trouble!

'Guess they didn't stay in the saloon long after all,' he grimaced.

'They're riding fast!' said Billy Joe. 'They're gonna catch us!'

'We got to get to McVie's ranch before they do!' said Jess urgently and he flicked the reins and yelled in his horse's ear to make it go faster.

Billy Joe's body ached from the ride, and he groaned at the thought of going even faster and giving it even more pain, but the thought of Brickman and the two gunmen bearing down on them made him push Harvey harder.

Suddenly an awful thought hit him. He and Jess were within shooting range. If the gunmen started firing at them, the gunfire would spook the cattle and start them stampeding. The boys and their horses would be crushed beneath those hooves and speared by those long horns! Billy Joe only hoped the gunmen were clever enough to realise that if a stampede started, they'd be in just as much danger themselves. Brickman seemed dangerously shrewd, but Mack and Sandy appeared stupid enough to do something that crazy.

The two boys rode faster, driving their horses on. They reached the long driveway down towards the ranch house, the horses still galloping.

Please don't let Harvey step into a hole, or I'll break my neck! prayed Billy Joe.

Behind them the hoofbeats of the three gunmen's horses were getting ever closer. The boys had passed through the herd of cattle now, and when they had almost reached the ranch house, Billy Joe felt a buzz past his ear and heard the sound of a gun firing behind him. They were being shot at!

Billy Joe and Jess ducked as low as they could, lying almost flat on their horses' backs, urging the animals forward. Bullets flew around them. Suddenly Harvey stumbled and fell, and Billy Joe found himself flying up into the air and hurtling over the falling horse's head.

I'm gonna die! he thought.

Instinctively he tucked his head in towards his chest, bringing his arms and legs up so he was curling into a ball. He hit the ground on his shoulder and rolled and rolled and kept rolling, his arms and legs smashing into the ground as he did so.

Jess pulled up his horse and jumped down, running to Billy Joe.

Billy Joe lay face down on the ground. His body ached. Was anything broken? Surely his arms and legs must be.

He looked towards Harvey. The horse lay on the ground, whinnying and kicking with three of its legs. The fourth, one of its hind legs, stuck out at a painful angle, and blood ran down from its haunches from where it had been shot.

Jess knelt beside Billy Joe.

'Don't move, Billy Joe!' he commanded. 'If there's anything broke it'll make it worse!'

The three gunmen pulled their horses to a halt beside the two boys, and jumped down from their horses. Sandy and Mack had their guns drawn and pointed at Jess and Billy Joe.

'Time to die, boys!' rasped Mack.

CHAPTER 17

'Hold it!' barked a voice.

They all turned.

Colonel McVie was coming out of the ranch house and heading towards them.

'What's going on?' he demanded.

'These two were comin' here to kill you, Colonel,' said Brickman. 'They saw me and the boys were in town, and thought it would be a good time to come out and get you on your own.'

'We weren't comin' here to kill anyone!' said Jess angrily. 'We ain't even got guns!'

'No?' queried Brickman. He pointed to the roll of cloth tied to the saddle on the injured Harvey. 'What's in that bunk-roll, Injun-boy? Tell the Colonel.'

'Leave him alone!' shouted Jess. 'Can't you see he's hurt? Possibly he's broke somethin', comin' off that horse the way he did!'

McVie looked at the fallen horse and glared at the three gunmen.

'Who shot that horse?' he demanded.

'I did, Colonel,' said Sandy. 'We was tryin' to stop 'em gettin' to you!'

Jess watched anxiously as Billy Joe pushed himself up from the ground. Slowly, carefully, he began to flex his arms and legs; then his fingers. He ached all over his body, and he'd be badly bruised, but nothing was broken.

'Are these the boys that took your guns off you?' McVie demanded of Mack and Sandy.

'That's them right enough, Colonel,' nodded Mack. 'Like I say, they're killers, sure as sure.'

'One of his own gang told us that the Injun shot a man right between the eyes just a short while ago,' added Sandy. 'And it turns out to be true. We checked while we was in town. This here's Billy Joe Ford, the notorious killer.'

'I ain't no Injun and I ain't no killer!' responded Billy Joe angrily. Why were people saying that all the time? 'We just come here to talk to Colonel McVie!'

'Is that so?' demanded McVie.

Jess nodded.

'It sure is, Colonel.'

McVie narrowed his eyes thoughtfully.

'In that case, you'd better come in.'

'Colonel!' protested Brickman. 'These boys are dangerous!'

'Mr Brickman, I'm forty-eight years old,' said McVie. 'In my time I've fought Indians, rustlers, and Yankee soldiers. If I can't face two boys then I ain't the man I thought I was.' To Billy Joe he said. 'Anything broken?'

Billy Joe pushed himself to his feet, checking his body. Then he shook his head.

'No,' he said. 'Leastways, I don't think so.'

'Then you'd best come inside.'

Brickman scowled. 'I don't like it, Colonel,' he said. 'I'm in charge of security here. I should be with you and these boys.'

McVie looked at Jess and Billy Joe.

'You boys got any objection to that?'

Inwardly, Billy Joe did. *This man's a lying killer. I don't want him anywhere near us while we're telling you about him and his gunmen.* But Jess merely nodded.

'We got nothin' to hide, Colonel,' he said. 'Anythin' we got to say we can say in the open.'

'Then you can join us, Mr Brickman,' McVie announced. 'But first, let's see about this horse your men shot.'

He strode over to where Harvey lay, struggling and panting, and whinnying in pain. McVie sighed and shook his head sadly.

'Back leg's broke,' he said. He turned on the three cowboys and snapped at them angrily, 'Because of you, we gotta put this animal down! I sure hate to do that, but it's the only decent thing to do.' To Mack and Sandy, he ordered, 'You two. Put this horse out of its misery. Then get rid of it and get another one from the stable for this boy.'

'But Colonel –' protested Mack.

'There ain't no excuse for killin' a perfectly good horse!' snapped McVie angrily. 'An' I ain't never owed anyone' anythin' in my life! That horse died on my land by the hand of one of my men! That means I gotta replace it. So get another one from the stable and swap over the saddles.'

'Yes, Colonel,' muttered Mack.

'And make sure that boy's gun stays with the saddle.'

'But Colonel!' protested Sandy. 'They took our guns! He owes us our guns!'

McVie shook his head.

'You lost your guns in a fair situation,' said McVie. 'If you take that gun it'll be stealin'. That gun better be on that saddle when these boys come out.'

The two gunmen exchanged sullen looks, but nodded.

'OK, Colonel,' they said.

'Right,' McVie said to Jess and Billy Joe. 'Follow me.'

As the two boys followed McVie into his ranch-house, with Brickman following, Billy Joe and Jess exchanged puzzled glances. With what he'd said so far,

Colonel McVie seemed to be acting fair and honest, just like Deputy Stevens had said, which didn't fit with what had happened to Adam Holtz. Unless Brickman and his men had been acting on their own when they killed Adam, and not on McVie's orders. But why would Brickman do that?

As they walked into the main room, Jess heard the gunshot from outside and knew Harvey was dead. He was filled with dread about how he'd have to tell Jack that Harvey had been shot once they got back to the Ambersons. It was obvious from Jack's face that he loved that horse.

Billy Joe also was worried about how they were going to break the news to Jack about Harvey being killed, but right now, as they walked into McVie's house, his strongest feeling was one of awe. He'd never seen any place that looked so rich in his whole life. Even the saloons he'd been in with his Pa had never looked as expensive this.

A huge chandelier hung from the ceiling in the centre of the room. The walls were adorned with decorations: shields and arrows taken from Indians and the heads of animals the Colonel had obviously hunted. Paintings in gold frames hung on the walls, mostly paintings of Wild West life, with cowboys herding cattle or fighting Indians.

The chairs looked to be made of thick wood with deep red leather cushions.

Billy Joe reckoned Colonel McVie must be the richest person he'd ever met.

McVie sat down in one of the expensive-looking chairs and turned to Jess and Billy Joe. Brickman stood by, his face wearing a grim expression.

'OK,' said McVie curtly. 'Say what you gotta say.'

'We're callin' because Billy Joe here said when you came to the Ambersons' the other day, you seemed an honest man,' said Jess. 'Straight.'

Billy Joe frowned, puzzled. He hadn't said anything like that to Jess. And then he realised that Jess was playing McVie, buttering him up. McVie said nothing, just listened, but the boys could tell he was pleased at Jess's words.

'Which gets me wonderin' why an honest and straight man would link up with murderers like Brickman here and his men.'

'Now you listen here –' snarled Brickman, striding forward, his hand outstretched towards Jess ready to grab him.

'Wait!' ordered McVie, and Brickman stopped, but the anger on his face was plain to see.

'No one calls me a murderer to my face and gets away with it, Colonel. Kid or no kid.'

'I was there when you shot Adam, Holtz,' said Jess defiantly. 'He had no gun nor knife nor weapon of any kind on him. You shot an unarmed man.'

McVie threw a look at Brickman.

'You told me he was going for a weapon,' he said.

'That's what it looked like to me,' nodded Brickman. 'And my men will bear me out. I couldn't see if it was a knife or a gun he was goin' for, all I saw was him reaching round behind him.'

'You're a liar!' snapped Jess. 'Anyone could see he never had a gunbelt on. And there was no knife.'

Brickman's eyes narrowed.

'You ought to think careful before you call me or any man a liar, boy,' he snarled. 'That sort of talk can get someone shot.'

'I ain't afraid of you,' said Jess standing tall. 'You can only shoot unarmed men. And I know you're gonna get away with it, because the Deputy in Drygulch told me so. Me and Billy Joe came here today because we wanted Colonel McVie to know just what sort of low lives he's hiring.'

McVie growled, an angry rumbling sound.

'I don't appreciate people comin' in to my house and making false accusations about people who work for me,' he said warningly.

'They're not false,' said Jess. 'And that ain't all I come here to say.'

'If it's more accusations . . .' began McVie, starting to get up.

'Nope,' said Jess. 'It's this business of the cattle being stolen. How d'you know that it was Adam Holtz who took 'em.' He was looking at Brickman.

'I found 'em with Holtz's brand on,' said Brickman.

'You seen 'em, Colonel?' Jess asked. 'These cattle with Holtz's brand?'

'I don't need to,' said McVie. 'If Mr Brickman here says he's seen them, that's good enough for me.'

'The Ambersons and Holtz have been losin' cattle, too,' said Billy Joe hotly. 'Maybe they got your brand on 'em now?'

McVie glared at Billy Joe.

'Are you accusing me of cattle rustlin'?' he demanded, his voice low and threatening.

'Well someone's stealin' cattle, and it ain't the Ambersons. And it sure weren't Adam Holtz,' said Billy Joe. Jess rolled his eyes – when would his friend learn how to handle situations like this?

McVie pointed towards the door. His finger, like the rest of his big body, was shaking with anger.

'Get out!' he ordered.

'He ain't sayin' it's you, Colonel. He – both of us – are just sayin' you ought to watch who you got workin' for you,' said Jess.

McVie turned to Brickman, his fury obvious.

'Brickman, get these boys out of my sight now! And I don't want to see them on my property again!'

'No problem, Colonel,' nodded Brickman.

He grabbed Jess and Billy Joe roughly by their arms, his fingers digging into their flesh, making both boys wince. Jess banged the knuckles of his free hand hard on the back of Brickman's fist, making Brickman let him go with an oath of pain.

'We can walk,' said Jess. 'We don't need to be dragged anywhere.'

Brickman threw a look at McVie, who nodded, and Brickman let go of Billy Joe's arm.

'Go with 'em, though,' said McVie. 'Make sure they leave. I don't want them sneakin' back causin' trouble.'

Brickman nodded and followed Jess and Billy Joe as they headed for the door. When they reached the outside, Mack and Sandy were waiting.

'What happened?' asked Sandy.

'These boys are leavin',' said Brickman. 'They told Colonel lies about us, and the Colonel didn't believe them.'

Sandy and Mack grinned.

'See?' smirked Mack. 'We're lawmen. No way the Colonel's gonna believe you against us.'

'This ain't over yet,' Jess told him.

'This part is,' said Brickman. 'But before you go, let me give you one final warning. The Colonel's lettin' you walk out of here. If it was me, I'd have shot you both dead for callin' me what you did. So hear this. Next time we meet up, the Colonel may not be around. And when that happens, you're both dead. I don't care what excuse I have to use, but I ain't gonna have you two goin' around talkin' about me like that without doin' somethin' about it.'

'You can try,' said Jess calmly. 'Come on, Billy Joe.'

Jess's horse was tethered to the rail where he had left it. Next to it was another horse, black and white, with Billy Joe's saddle on it, just as McVie had ordered. Also, as McVie had ordered, Billy Joe's roll with his pistol in it had been left fixed to the saddle.

The dead body of Harvey had gone, but there was a patch of blood where he had fallen, and flies were already buzzing around the spot.

The two boys walked to the horses and untethered them from the rail, feeling Brickman's furious eyes on them.

'Think he's gonna shoot us?' whispered Billy Joe.

'Not right at this minute,' muttered Jess. 'I reckon he's too scared of upsettin' the Colonel to do it on his land. But let's hope he don't follow us.'

The two boys mounted up and rode away. All the time they were aware of Brickman, Sandy and Mack standing watching them, their hands on the butts of their pistols.

CHAPTER 18

At the Ambersons', the small ranch was in a state of tension. Mr Amberson paced around the yard at the front, scanning the horizon for any sign of Jess and Billy Joe. Shane, Andy and Jack sat on the porch and watched him. Patch bounced around the yard, following Amberson as he paced.

Whether it was the tension, or the heat, or the general worry, Manda had gestured and signed that she felt tired, and Mrs Amberson had helped her to bed and tucked her in. Although Mrs Amberson gave her daughter a big smile and a hug, once outside Manda's bedroom, Mrs Amberson had to bite her lip to stop herself moaning out loud with the unhappiness that filled her over her daughter's condition. The doctors in Chicago had said the clean air out in the West would help Manda, but so far Manda had just got paler and thinner. She was wasting away, and there seemed to be nothing anyone could do to save her.

In the front of the house, Mr Amberson headed for the porch.

'Jess and Billy Joe should have been back by now,' he said, worried. 'D'you think something's happened to them?'

'J-Jess and B-Billy J-Joe can take c-care of th-themselves,' said Shane confidently. 'Ain't that r-r-right, Andy?'

'It sure is!' nodded Andy. 'Jess is tough, and Billy Joe is great with a gun!'

'Not against a killer like Brickman,' sighed Amberson.

Mrs Amberson appeared from the house.

'Any sign of them?' she asked.

'Not yet,' sighed Amberson, shaking his head.

'Y-yes!' cried Shane. His keen eyes had spotted a cloud of dust approaching. Two horses.

'It might be Brickman and his men!' said Mrs Amberson, alarmed.

'N-no,' said Shane. 'Th-they w-wouldn't be riding f-fast l-like th-that j-just to c-come here.'

'Shane's right,' agreed Amberson. 'It's got to be Jess and Billy Joe.'

As the horses drew nearer they saw it was indeed Jess and Billy Joe, but they were surprised to see that Billy Joe was riding a different horse from the one he'd been riding when he left.

'What happened to Harvey?' demanded Jack, as Jess and Billy Joe got off their horses.

Jess looked at the small boy and shook his head.

'I'm afraid he's dead, Jack,' he said. 'One of Brickman's men shot him.'

Jack's face crumpled, and he began to cry, tears coursing down his cheeks. Mrs Amberson put her arm around her son and hugged him into her dress.

'Better come inside, Jack,' she said softly. 'I'll fix you something.'

She shook her head sadly at the boys, and led the crying Jack towards the house. Jess and Billy Joe looked after them, feeling awful.

'I'm sorry, Mr Amberson,' said Billy Joe. 'We didn't mean for it to happen. Brickman and his men were chasin' us, and they shot Harvey right out from under me.'

Mr Amberson nodded, the expression on his face a mixture of sadness and anger.

'I'm just glad they didn't shoot either of you,' he said, patting their shoulders.

'They were going to,' said Jess. 'But McVie came out and stopped them.'

They told Amberson, Shane and Andy about their conversation in town with Deputy Stevens and about their confrontation with McVie at his ranch.

'That was very brave of you,' said Amberson. 'But dangerous. You were taking a big chance.'

'I thought it was a chance worth takin',' said Jess. 'I thought we should let McVie know what kind of killers he was employin'.' He looked down at the ground unhappily. 'I guess we just made things worse. Not only did we get Harvey killed, we riled McVie.'

'He was already riled up,' said Amberson ruefully.

'If you don't mind my saying so, Mr Amberson, I think we need to ride out and keep an eye on your herd, just in case Brickman or any of his men try and steal 'em,' suggested Jess.

'You could be right,' grunted Amberson. 'Adam Holtz said he'd lost cattle. McVie could well send Brickman to do the same to us . . .'

He was cut off by Mrs Amberson yelling 'William! William! Quickly!'

The note of panic in her voice made them all break into a run towards the house. Mrs Amberson had come to the doorway, and as Amberson and the boys reached it she turned and ran back inside, heading for the bedrooms at the back. They followed her.

'I was with Jack when I heard a crash from Manda's room . . .' she told them, and they could tell she was doing her best to keep herself under control and not start screaming.

She pushed the bedroom door open and they saw Manda lying on the floor, her body racked with coughs. Jack was kneeling beside her, his face showing fear and panic, as he looked at his sister.

Blood smeared the front of Manda's dress and stained the rug beneath her head. As Manda gave another violent cough, blood gushed out from her mouth.

CHAPTER 19

The boys looked shocked. Mr Amberson had already rushed to his daughter, lifting her up.

'We have to get her to the doctor's in town!' he said.

'I'm coming with you!' said Mrs Amberson, grabbing up clothes and stuffing them into a bag.

'Shane, Billy Joe, Andy. Go and get the buggy ready!' said Jess. 'Put two horses on it. It'll go faster.'

The three boys nodded and hurried out.

Mr Amberson had lifted Manda onto the bed and was bending her forwards to make sure all the blood she coughed up came out and didn't go back down her throat where she could choke on it. Manda was deathly pale. Her eyes were open, but they had rolled up into her head so they could only see the whites of her eyes.

Mrs Amberson had grabbed up a blanket and was wrapping it around Manda, while Mr Amberson held her upright. Then he let Manda sink back against him.

'You all go to town,' said Jess. 'Take Jack as well. We'll look after things here.'

'And if Brickman comes . . . ?' began Mr Amberson.

'Forget Brickman!' snapped Mrs Amberson. 'Our daughter is dying!'

'I'm sure she'll be all right, ma'am,' said Jess. 'Doc Benson is a good doctor.'

Even as he said it, Jess knew he was just saying the words to try and make them feel better. The way Manda looked, coughing up so much blood that way, she was not going to be all right at all. And Doc Benson was OK at fixing everyday things, like a broken arm or even taking a bullet out of someone. But this was something different. This was really bad.

The boys stood and watched and waved goodbye as the Ambersons set off for Drygulch in the buggy. Mr Amberson was on the driving seat with Jack, and Mrs Amberson was in the back with Manda, wrapped up in a blanket and propped up to make sure she didn't choke to death. She was still unconscious.

'She gonna die, Jess?' asked Andy.

'N-no!' put in Shane firmly. 'Sh-she ain't gonna die! Doc B-Benson will s-save her!'

Jess and Billy Joe exchanged glances. Manda was in a bad way. There was a chance she wouldn't even survive the fifteen mile journey into town, and both boys knew it.

'What are we gonna do, Jess?' asked Billy Joe.

'We do what we said we was gonna do,' said Jess. 'We go and check on Mr Amberson's cattle. Make sure no one steals 'em. After all, he's payin' us to work for him. So that's what we'll do.'

'A-all of us?' asked Shane.

Jess nodded. 'It's getting late, so we'll set out at first light tomorrow. And from now on we stay together. You, me and Billy Joe will take us a horse each. Andy can ride with me.'

'You gonna take Mr Pedersen's rifle?' asked Billy Joe.

Jess hesitated.

'I don't know, Billy Joe,' he said, unsure.

'It seems to me if we run up against some armed killers, we're gonna need somethin' more than rocks to throw at them if we're gonna come out alive,' said Billy Joe.

'He's r-right, J-Jess,' added Shane. 'I don't l-like g-guns any more th-than you do, Jess. You know I d-d-don't, b-but . . .'

Jess sighed.

'I guess you're right,' he said. He added sharply to Andy. 'But you don't touch it, you hear, Andy! I don't want you shootin' someone by mistake.'

Andy nodded, then frowned. 'What about Patch?'

At the mention of his name Patch came bounding up to the four boys, wagging his tail.

'Patch has got four legs,' said Jess. 'He can walk.'

'He'll get tired,' complained Andy.

'No he won't,' said Jess. 'Anyway, Patch has gotta start earnin' his livin' same as the rest of us.'

CHAPTER 20

Night fell. The boys had decided they couldn't trust Brickman and his men not to come out to the ranch.

'We're gonna have to take turns keeping watch,' Jess said. 'I'll take first watch. Billy Joe and Shane take second watch.'

'What about me?' demanded Andy. 'I can keep watch as well.'

'We got a long ride tomorrow,' said Jess. 'You're the littlest and you're gonna need your sleep.'

'I wanna keep watch as well,' insisted Andy.

Jess looked at Billy Joe and Shane and sighed.

'OK,' he said. 'You can take first watch with me.'

Andy smiled.

'I'll keep my eyes an' ears sharp, Jess!' he promised.

Jess turned to Shane and Billy Joe.

'You two grab some shut-eye now,' he said. 'I'll wake you when it's time to change over.'

Billy Joe pulled off his boots and lay down on the bed. He didn't take his clothes off. He wanted to be ready to spring into action if anything bad happened. Shane was obviously tired, and soon Billy Joe heard him snoring. But Billy Joe couldn't sleep. There was too much going on in his mind. He was remembering being chased by Brickman and his two gunmen, Harvey being shot and killed, and the threats from Sandy and Mack. Then there was Manda coughing up all that blood. She was going to die, Billy Joe was sure of it. What would happen to the Ambersons then? Would they still stay here? Or would they go back to Chicago? If they packed up and returned to the East, why were Billy Joe and the rest of the gang putting their lives at risk defending this ranch and the Ambersons' cattle?

I ain't never gonna get to sleep tonight, thought Billy Joe. *I'm gonna be wide awake when Jess wakes me up to take my watch, and I'm gonna be awake all through keeping watch. I'm gonna be in no fit state for anything tomorrow.*

✳ ✳ ✳

'Wake up, Billy Joe.'

It was Jess, shaking him. Billy Joe had fallen asleep after all, even though it felt like he hadn't. Shane was already awake and pulling his boots on.

Billy Joe struggled up and began putting on his boots. Then he shrugged his jacket on and tugged it close around him. The night air was cold.

He looked across at the bed and saw that Andy was curled up on it, fast asleep.

'When did Andy fall asleep?' he asked quietly.

Jess grinned.

'About ten minutes after we started keepin' watch,' he replied. 'But don't you tell him that.'

'W-we w-won't,' whispered Shane.

Jess pulled off his boots and crawled onto the bed.

'It's all been quiet out there so far,' he said. 'But that don't mean anythin'. Keep your ears open.'

'Will do,' nodded Billy Joe, and he headed for the porch. Outside was the best place to keep watch. That way he'd hear every last little sound.

He settled himself down on the bench on the porch. Soon after, Shane joined him. The two boys sat, looking out at the night sky and the vast prairie. Above them, the black sky was filled with the twinkling lights of stars. There were hundreds of them. Maybe thousands.

'That's s-some b-big sky,' said Shane.

'Sure is,' agreed Billy Joe.

'Wh-what you reckon st-stars is made of, Billy Joe?' asked Shane.

'I don't rightly know,' admitted Billy Joe. 'Guess that's why people like us need schoolin' to teach us things.'

The two boys fell silent, looking up at the vast expanse of sky. It was no longer just black, but glittering with lights.

'Lookin' at that big sky, we sure is small when you think about it,' muttered Billy Joe.

They sat and looked up at the stairs and listened to the sounds of the night. There was the sound of the night wind whistling over the range and through the trees. Night animals scuttling and slinking through the brush and the grass. But no heavy sounds. No horses' hooves or the sound of boots or guns being cocked. Nothing for miles.

CHAPTER 21

The night remained quiet. No visits from Brickman or McVie or any of his men.

Next morning the boys fixed breakfast, then Shane wrote a note which he fixed to the door of the ranch house.

'What's that note say?' asked Billy Joe.

'It s-says we g-gone out ch-checkin' cattle,' said Shane. 'It's in case the Ambersons c-come b-back before w-we get b-back. Or in c-case the Sheriff c-calls.'

'Good thinkin',' nodded Jess.

They packed up their bedrolls and enough food and water to see them over two days, then set off. Jess rode with Andy squashed behind him on the saddle, and Pedersen's rifle near to his right hand. Shane rode old Ruby and Billy Joe his black and white horse that McVie had given him. Patch seemed happy enough to trot and run along beside the horses.

They kept to the fenceline that bordered the Ambersons' ranch, and soon came upon the herd of steers grazing.

'There ain't as many as I thought there'd be,' commented Billy Joe.

'No, there ain't,' agreed Jess, frowning. 'Mr Amberson reckoned he had a hundred head of cattle. Let's count 'em.'

The boys each walked their horses through the herd, counting slowly and carefully as they did so.

'S-seventy,' reported Shane when they re-grouped.

'That's what I made it,' said Billy Joe.

'Me too,' said Jess.

'Me too,' said Andy, although the truth was he'd stopped counting after ten because he used his fingers and had run out.

'H-how'd they g-get them out?' asked Shane. 'We rode along the f-fence and it ain't b-been c-cut.'

'Not yet,' said Jess. 'Let's follow it some more.'

They rode on, staying along the fence the whole time. After two miles of riding they found a place where the wire between the fences had been cut and pulled back. The ground between the two posts had been trampled.

'This is where they took 'em.' said Jess.

Billy Joe looked at the trampled ground, and the trail of hoof tracks that led away from the fence.

'Reckon we ought to follow 'em?' he suggested.

'It's the only way to find out where they went,' said Jess.

'I b-bet they take us to M-McVie's ranch!' Shane said, excited.

'Maybe we ought to go and get the Sheriff?' suggested Andy.

Jess shook his head.

'The Deputy told us the Sheriff ain't got no jurisdiction out here, Andy,' he said. 'But if these tracks lead us to McVie's ranch, we can face him with it. The Ambersons' cattle will be there with their brand on.'

'If we do that, McVie will kill us,' said Billy Joe.

'I ain't so sure,' said Jess thoughtfully. 'If he wanted to kill us he could have done so before now. But he let us go. I got a hunch that his man, Brickman, is usin' McVie and his ranch for some private cattle rustlin'.'

Billy Joe shook his head.

'Ain't nothin' happens at McVie's ranch he don't know about,' he said. 'If there's stolen cattle there, you can bet McVie's in on it.'

'The Deputy said McVie was honest and straight, Billy Joe,' Jess pointed out.

'The Deputy ain't got the brains of a frog,' grunted Billy Joe.

'That may be, but I still think we have to follow these tracks and find out where Mr Amberson's cattle are,' said Jess. 'It may be dangerous. We know Brickman and his men are killers. So if you don't want to come with me, that's fine. You can just wait back at the ranch and tell the Ambersons where I went and about the missin' cattle when they come back.'

Shane shook his head.

'You ain't g-goin' after 'em, w-without me, Jess!' he said firmly.

'Nor me!' piped up Andy from behind Jess.

Jess nodded, and looked at Billy Joe.

'Billy Joe?' he asked.

'If you run into trouble you're gonna need all the help you can get, Jess,' nodded Billy Joe, then added with a grin, 'And I'm a better shot than you.'

'W-what we gonna do w-with Patch?' asked Shane.

The dog barked on hearing his name and looked up at the boys.

'We can't leave him here!' protested Andy.

'No, I guess we can't,' agreed Jess. 'But we don't want him barkin' an' runnin' ahead of us. That could get dangerous.' He thought for a moment, then got down from his horse and whistled. Patch came bouncing over to him. Jess tied the end of a rope loosely around Patch's neck, and looped the other end through a buckle on his saddle. He gave the end to Andy.

'You hang on to that, Andy,' he ordered. 'If Patch looks like he's gonna run off, you pull him back and make him behave. OK?'

'I sure will, Jess,' nodded Andy.

Jess got back onto his horse.

'OK, boys,' he said. 'Let's go catch us some rustlers.'

CHAPTER 22

They followed the tracks of the Ambersons' cattle for about seven miles. To their surprise, the tracks moved away from the direction that would take them to McVie's ranch, and headed towards a point where the plain became woodland, then went up into the foothills of the mountains.

'Huh. Looks like it ain't McVie after all,' commented Billy Joe.

'Th-then who is it?' asked Shane.

'Maybe it's Indians?' suggested Andy.

Jess shook his head.

'Not these,' he said. 'Those are cowboy's horses – you can see tracks of their metal shoes.'

The boys looked towards the foothills. There were no signs of any cattle on the plain between them and the woods and the mountains.

'They must've hidden them in those woods,'

suggested Billy Joe, but Shane shook his head.

'Cattle n-need grazin' to eat,' he said. 'There's not much in the woods.'

'They won't need much grazin',' Jess pointed out. 'They only took thirty of Mr Amberson's cattle.'

'But say they were the same ones who took Adam Holtz's cattle,' pointed out Billy Joe. 'They'd need space for all them, sure enough.'

'Good point,' nodded Jess.

'Maybe there's more g-grass in the f-foothills,' suggested Shane.

'Only one way to find out,' said Jess. 'But be careful. If you see anyone comin', pretend we're just out ridin'.'

'R-ridin' where?' asked Shane.

'Explorin'.' added Jess. 'That's what they call it when you go somewhere you ain't never been before. An' that's what we're doin' right now if we're asked.'

* * *

The boys followed the cattle tracks through the brush and woodland, until the tracks headed towards an opening in the high rock walls of the foothills.

'I think we oughta be careful about goin' through there,' cautioned Billy Joe. 'We don't know what's ahead. Could be cattle, could be rustlers.'

Reining his horse in, Jess chewed his lip and frowned thoughtfully.

'I think you're right, Billy Joe,' he said. 'We need to scout ahead careful-like.'

He gestured for Shane to follow them to a place where the trees were thickest and they all dismounted.

Jess tied his horse's reins to a branch of a tree, and Shane and Billy Joe did the same.

'OK,' said Jess, 'here's what we're gonna do. Me and Billy Joe are gonna climb up that slope there and get a good view of what lies ahead. Shane, you stay here with Andy and Patch and the horses. Do your best to keep 'em quiet.'

Shane nodded.

Jess turned to Andy and said firmly, 'Andy, you do whatever Shane tells you. You're not to go sneakin' off anywhere.'

'I don't sneak off!' protested Andy.

Jess was about to give Andy examples of when he did just that, but decided this wasn't the time to start arguing.

'And make sure that you keep Patch with you,' he warned. 'We don't know what's beyond here. If it's bad guys, they might kill Patch if he goes after them.'

Andy knelt down and hugged Patch close, the string wrapped around his fingers.

'I'll keep him here,' he promised.

'OK,' said Jess. To Shane he added, 'One last thing, if you hear shootin', don't wait for us. Put Andy on a horse and you an' him ride out of here as fast as you can.'

Shane shook his head.

'I w-won't leave w-without you,' he said firmly.

'Yes you will,' Jess told him equally firmly. 'No sense in all four us gettin' killed.'

'We ain't gettin' killed,' put in Billy Joe, worried that Andy might get scared.

'Not if we're careful,' nodded Jess.

Jess and Billy Joe headed towards a narrow track that led to some rocks and scrub that went up into the foothills of the mountains. Jess carried his rifle in one hand. Billy Joe stuck his pistol in the waistband of his trousers.

The climb up was made harder because they were determined not to make any noise, which meant going slow and making sure they didn't slip. Finally, they got to a level rocky plateau. With Jess in the lead, they crawled on their hands and knees across the rocks, until they came to an overhang where the rocks fell away from them. Below them was a valley.

No, thought Billy Joe, *it's not really a valley. There's only one way in and out*. It was a huge grassy area with rock walls all the way round, and the only way in or out was the narrow entrance in the rocks that the boys had seen earlier.

What Jess and Billy Joe saw in the valley below made them glad they hadn't gone through that rocky gap. The whole area was filled with cattle. There were about ten horses tethered to trees at one side of the valley, near to where a small fire was burning.

'There's got to be a couple of hundred steers there,' said Billy Joe, awed.

'It's the stolen cattle all right,' said Jess. 'See the different brands? That's Amberson's. And those are Adam Holtz's. The others must be McVie's.'

'They're re-brandin' 'em,' said Billy Joe, and he motioned towards the fire. A cowboy was crouched there, holding a branding iron in the hot coals, with a cloth wrapped round the handle to protect his hands from the heat. Jess let out a gasp of recognition.

'It's Sandy!' he said.

'And there's the other one. Mack,' said Billy Joe, pointing at a pair of cowboys bringing a steer towards the fire.

Jess nodded grimly.

'Most of 'em here was with Brickman when he shot Adam, as well,' he said. He studied the other cowboys, some of whom were riding their horses among the cattle, sorting out those that needed branding. 'Yeah, for sure. I recognise a few of the others.'

'Some of 'em were with him when he came out with McVie to see Mrs Amberson,' said Billy Joe. 'And now we got 'em fair and square.'

'Not yet we ain't,' said Jess. He made his mind up. 'We got to go tell Shane and Andy.'

The two boys moved away from the edge of the overhang and moved swiftly back across the rocky plateau, then slid down through the brush-filled slope, keeping low.

Shane, Andy and Patch were waiting for them in the trees. Briefly, Jess and Billy Joe told them what they'd seen.

'Me and Billy Joe need to stay here and keep watch on 'em,' said Jess, 'just in case they move the cattle somewheres else, so we can follow them. Shane, we need you to ride into Drygulch. The Sheriff ought to be back by now. Tell him we need him to come out here urgent and tell him why.'

'But Deputy Stevens said the Sheriff ain't got no authority outside of town,' Billy Joe pointed out.

'That's true,' said Jess. 'But when the Sheriff hears about this, I'm pretty sure he's gonna come runnin'. An' he'll bring a posse with him.' Turning back to Shane, Jess said, 'You're the best rider here, Shane. Think you can get to Drygulch quick?'

Shane nodded.

'T-trust me, J-Jess,' he said.

'Better go out through the trees first,' suggested Jess. 'We don't want the rustlers spottin' you. Then you can ride hard once you reach the open range. Take my horse – he's a lot faster than Ruby.'

'Probably cos he's younger!' Billy Joe muttered and Shane and the others smiled.

Shane untied Jess's horse and led it away through the trees.

'What you want me an' Patch to do, Jess?' asked Andy eagerly.

Jess and Bill Joe exchanged concerned looks. The problem with Andy was that he would walk into trouble without thinking of the danger. He'd done it before.

'Tell you what, while me and Billy Joe get back there and watch what's goin' on, you an' Patch stay here and look after the horses,' said Jess.

'That ain't no fun!' Andy complained. 'I want to see the bad guys!'

'None of this is fun, Andy,' said Jess seriously. 'These men are thieves and killers. Someone's got to stay here and look after our horses and keep 'em from strayin'. If we have to make a run for it in a hurry, we don't want to come down and find the horses are gone, do we?'

Andy thought about it.

'No,' he agreed. 'So it's an important job?'

'It sure is, Andy,' said Jess. 'We're countin' on you and Patch to do it right.'

'OK,' nodded Andy. 'We'll stay here and watch the horses. Won't we, Patch?'

With that, Andy went to where the two horses were tied to the branch of a tree, and sat down on a fallen log near them, trailing Patch on the string behind him.

Jess and Billy Joe began to scramble up the slope

towards the overhang again. Jess held the rifle, and Billy Joe his pistol.

'If you ask me, we should've tied Andy and Patch to a tree,' muttered Billy Joe as they crept along through the scrub. 'They're more likely to go strayin' than either of those horses.'

CHAPTER 23

Jess and Billy Joe lay on the overhang, watching the cowboys selecting steers one after the other and taking them to the fire. There, they threw the steer down and hog-tied its legs with a rope while the cowboy with the branding iron changed the brand on its flank. Once that was done, the cowboys let the steer up.

Because there were a lot of animals, and some were harder to catch, throw down and hog-tie than others, the procedure took a long time.

'I sure hope Andy isn't gettin' restless down there,' murmured Billy Joe.

'He'll be OK,' murmured back Jess. 'He's got Patch to look after.'

'That dog's as bad as he is,' grunted Billy Joe. 'Think Shane's got to Drygulch yet?'

'Hard to tell,' replied Jess. 'Shane rides good, but it

depends what he runs into on the way. I just hope the Sheriff's back.'

Suddenly they saw movement at the entrance to the valley.

'Someone's comin',' whispered Billy Joe urgently.

The boys looked, and saw a familiar figure dressed all in black riding his horse through the narrow entrance to the valley. It was Brickman. With him was another man, riding a white horse. This second man wore a Stetson that covered his face, but he also wore a grey suit, marking him as separate from the cowboys.

There was no urgency about the two men. They trotted their horses over to the fire where the others were re-branding the cattle, and both got down. Brickman then gestured at the cattle, and the man in the grey suit nodded. Although the boys couldn't hear what was being said from his distance, they could tell by the body language of the men that everything seemed to be going fine.

'That must be the guy who's buyin' the cattle from Brickman,' said Jess. 'My guess is he's makin' arrangements to have them moved somewhere else.'

Billy Joe strained to get a better look at the man in the suit.

'Well I'll be darned!' he breathed, astonished. 'You know who I think that is!'

Jess strained to see through the long grass. The man in grey finally took off his Stetson and turned, so now they could see his face clearly for the first time.

It was Mayor Redding!

'I knew he was a crook but I never figured him for a cattle rustler!' muttered Jess angrily.

The branding of the cattle looked as if it was almost finished. The last steer had just had its brand re-burned on its flank and it lurched to its feet.

'Looks to me like they finished brandin' 'em,' said Billy Joe. 'What are we gonna do if they start movin' out?'

'We follow 'em,' said Jess.

'But how're we gonna let Shane know which way we've gone?' asked Billy Joe.

'With a herd this size there should be big enough tracks for him to follow,' said Jess.

Suddenly a flicker of movement down in the valley caught Billy Joe's eyes, and he let out a gasp of anger.

'Darn it!'

Jess followed Billy Joe's gaze, and saw it too. Patch was working his way through the legs of the cattle, but the string on his neck was nowhere to be seen. Hurrying behind him was the small figure of Andy. Andy was obviously trying to hide as he moved, but he was also dead set on trying to catch Patch. 'I said we should've tied 'em both up!' groaned Billy Joe.

So far none of the cowboys in the valley had seen Andy or Patch. Jess got to his knees.

'I'll go catch 'em,' he said. 'You stay here.'

'You'll never catch 'em both on your own,' said Billy Joe, and he began to get up, too. He was stopped by Jess grabbing him.

'Wait!' whispered Jess. 'Look!'

Billy Joe looked.

Some of the steers had caught sight of Andy and were intrigued by this small boy. They ambled towards him, their heads lowered, their sharp horns threateningly close.

'They're gonna trample him!' whispered Billy Joe, shocked. 'Or gore him!'

Andy had stopped and was backing away, but behind him there was only the sheer rock wall of the valley.

Jess picked up the rifle and put it to his shoulder, aiming through the sight at the steer nearest to Andy.

'I'm gonna have to drop that steer,' said Jess. 'If he gets any closer he's gonna squash Andy against that cliff.'

'You sure you can kill that steer from here?' asked Billy Joe, concerned. 'If you only wound it, it's gonna go for Andy for sure.'

'If I don't it's gonna trample him anyways,' said Jess.

Suddenly there was the sound of barking from below. Patch had arrived beside Andy and had got between him and the nearest steers. He was standing protectively in front of Andy, barking and growling and baring his teeth at the cattle.

The sound of the dog barking made the cowboys and Redding look up, surprised. Billy Joe saw them reaching for their guns.

One steer looked down at the barking Patch, as if it was puzzled by this strange creature. The other steers also stood watching, equally curious.

Suddenly Patch leapt at the steer, mouth open, jaws gaping, growling fiercely and aiming for its face. The beast leapt back in alarm. Patch leapt again. The steer turned and ran. As it did so, the beasts nearest also turned. And then they were running, crashing and barging into one another in their desperation to get away from this dangerous animal.

'Stampede!' yelled one of the cowboys.

By now the feeling of panic had spread amongst most of the herd, and the cattle surged, heading for the entrance to the valley, which was the nearest escape from the snarling dog.

Jess kept his rifle aimed at the area around Andy and Patch, in case the cattle should stampede back, but it looked as if they were safe.

The same couldn't be said for the cowboys. The stampeding cattle crashed towards the fire, and Billy Joe saw four of the cowboys disappear beneath the pounding hooves. Desperately, Brickman and the other cowboys fired their guns at the cattle to try to head them away from the entrance to the valley. Other cowboys had jumped on their horses and were riding towards the valley entrance, also firing their guns to turn the cattle back. As the two boys watched one steer ran straight into one of the horses, its long horns driving into the side of the horse. The cowboy astride it lost his grip and fell, and then both cowboy and horse were trampled by the huge beasts.

By now the steers were in a state of panic and by sheer weight of numbers and their size they forced their way through the narrow entrance of the valley and out into the woodland beyond, crashing through trees and saplings.

'Catch 'em!' yelled Brickman desperately.

Three of the cowboys rode after the disappearing herd, chasing and trying to catch them.

The scene in the valley was one of carnage. Five of the cowboys lay still on the ground, trampled to death, the hot embers from the fire scattered by the stampeding cattle.

Mayor Redding had managed to find a hiding place behind a rock, and now he came out from behind it, looking shocked by what had happened.

Brickman stood, gun drawn, in the middle of the valley, looking around him in bewilderment as if he couldn't believe what he'd just seen. Mack stumbled over to join him, his gun also drawn, but there was no sign of Sandy. Then Brickman saw Andy and Patch standing small and defenceless against the rock wall of the valley. He swung his gun towards them.

'He's gonna shoot Andy!' whispered Billy Joe, horrified. 'Quick! Shoot Brickman first!'

Jess swung the rifle to his shoulder and took aim at Brickman. Billy Joe saw Jess's finger tighten on the trigger, and then release it again as Jess hesitated. Swiftly, desperate to save Andy, Billy Joe pulled his pistol from his belt, pointed it down into the valley at Brickman, and fired. His bullet kicked up dirt from the ground near the Marshal's boots.

Immediately, Brickman, Redding and Mack swung their attention towards the overhang, looking up and scanning the grassy area at the top of the valley.

'You up there!' shouted Brickman, his voice carrying. 'Whoever you are! Throw down your guns or I kill this kid!'

'I recognise him!' yelled the Mayor. 'He's one of that gang, always causing trouble in my town.'

Billy Joe and Jess peered through the undergrowth down into the valley. Brickman still had his gun pointed at Andy. Redding was beside him, a look of terror on his face. Mack glared upwards, his gun pointed up at the overhang.

'If you shoot him I'll kill you for sure!' shouted back Billy Joe.

'That'll be the other boys up there!' said the Mayor.

Brickman ignored him. Instead, he shouted up towards Jess and Billy Joe, 'Don't make me come lookin' for you! Throw down your guns!'

'Don't do it, Billy Joe!' shouted Andy. 'He'll kill you if you do!'

'I ain't sure if I can hit him from this distance with just a pistol, Jess,' muttered Billy Joe. 'That rifle of yours is the best thing we got.'

'I ain't sure, Billy Joe,' murmured Jess unhappily. 'If I shoot and miss, my guess is he'll kill Andy for sure. And if I hit him, I'm worried the other guy will shoot Andy before he comes after us.'

Once again Brickman shouted up.

'You listen up good, boys! This is how it's gonna be! Mack here is gonna point his gun at this little friend of yours here. I'm gonna come and find you. If Mack hears shooting – and it don't matter whether it's you shootin' at me or me shootin' at you – he's gonna blow holes in this little kid. So you'd better hand yourself over peaceful if you want him to stay alive.'

With that, Brickman slipped towards the entrance to the valley.

CHAPTER 24

The boys watched as Mack moved closer towards Andy, his gun pointed at the small boy. Mayor Redding remained standing in the valley, not far from Mack. Both boys could see that the Mayor was trembling and had a look of helplessness on his face. Andy stood small and defiant as he glared up at Mack. With one hand Andy held onto the fur at the back of Patch's neck, keeping a hold on the dog.

'What are we gonna do, Jess?' asked Billy Joe desperately.

Jess shook his head.

'When Brickman finds us, he's gonna be shootin' us,' he said. 'And when Mack hears his gun, he's gonna shoot Andy. So I guess we got nothin' to lose.' He sighed unhappily. 'I guess I have to shoot Mack first.'

He wriggled across the ground to be nearer the edge of the overhang. Then he put the rifle to his shoulder and aimed it down into the valley, towards Mack.

'Make sure you don't hit Andy,' warned Billy Joe.

'Shut up!' hissed back Jess. 'This is gonna be hard enough as it is, without you makin' it worse!'

Jess aimed the rifle and looked through the gunsight that ran along the barrel. *Aim for the biggest part of the target*, he told himself. That was the body. He didn't want to kill Mack. He'd never shot anybody in his whole life, but this situation would be death for all of them unless he did something. Certainly it would be death for Andy, and he wasn't going to let that happen. Not to little Andy.

The whole time he was listening for the sounds that would tell them Brickman was here. He wondered how long it would take the crooked Marshal to get to them? A long time, Jess hoped. He was sure he'd be careful, aware that the boys were armed.

Jess took a bead on Mack's chest. Mack was standing firm, his pistol still aimed rock-steady at Andy, although he kept shooting glances around the top edge of the valley wall.

'Any sign of 'em yet, Brick?' Mack called.

There was no response from Brickman. Billy Joe guessed the Marshal was staying quiet so as not to let the boys know his position. Billy Joe strained his ears, listening for the sound of undergrowth being trodden, or boots on rocks. Anything that would tell them how close Brickman was.

'Better do it soon, Jess!' Billy Joe urged. 'We gotta get out of here before Brickman gets to us!'

Jess ignored Billy Joe and kept his eyes on the figure of Mack through the gunsight. He was a long distance away. If he missed, then Mack would be sure to shoot. He had to get it right with this one shot!

Jess held the rifle as firmly as he could. If his hands shook even a little, it would throw his firing off. He gritted his teeth, kept his watch through the gunsight, and let his finger tighten on the trigger. *Squeeze, don't pull!* That was what he'd been told about firing a gun accurately. Pull the trigger and it makes the gun jump, then you'll miss. He felt a lump in his throat. Say he missed Mack and shot Andy instead?

'Hurry up!' urged Billy Joe.

He looked at Jess and saw the agony of indecision on his friend's face as he struggled to pull the trigger.

It's gonna have to be me who does it, thought Billy Joe. *Jess can't do this.* He held his pistol at arm's length, pointing it down into the valley, aimed at Mack. He closed one eye to get a better aim. He pulled, squeezing the trigger tighter . . .

BANG!

The shot echoed out. Mack stumbled back and fell. Redding leapt back and cowered, looking up towards the ridge.

Jess turned to look at Billy Joe, shocked.

'I got him!' said Billy Joe delightedly. And then his

face showed his shock as Mack pushed himself back to his feet. His left arm was hanging down by his side and blood was coming from his left shoulder, but his right hand was still holding his pistol.

'They shot me, Brick!' he yelled. 'I'm gonna show them what they get for doin' that!'

And he aimed the gun at Andy.

The next second Patch had torn himself away from Andy's grasp and leapt at Mack. And, as the boys watched, the dog sank his teeth deep into the cowboy's gun arm.

Mack shrieked and fell to the ground, with Patch on top of him. The boys saw Andy pick up a rock and rush towards Mack and Patch, and bring the rock down hard on Mack's injured shoulder, making the cowboy cry out in agony. Again, Andy lifted the rock and brought it down, this time on the cowboy's head knocking him out. All the time Patch was growling and snarling and biting at the writhing cowboy.

'Got you!'

The snarling triumphant voice behind them made Jess and Billy Joe turn. Brickman was standing there, his gun aimed at them.

Immediately Billy Joe swung his pistol at Brickman and pulled the trigger but there was just an empty click as the hammer fell. Either the pistol was empty, or the bullet had jammed!

'Jess!' he yelled in panic.

Jess hesitated, then his face hardened and he swung the rifle round, but Brickman fired first. Jess gave a yell and stumbled backwards, then Jess and the rifle disappeared over the rocky overhang.

CHAPTER 25

Billy Joe stared at the space where Jess had been, shocked. Jess dead? It wasn't possible.

Then he was aware that Brickman was sweeping his gun round to aim at him, and he threw himself to one side, just as Brickman fired. The bullet tore at his shirt and smashed into the rocks next to Billy Joe. His own gun was useless. Desperately, Billy Joe snatched up a small handful of rocks and threw them at Brickman and they hit the gunman in the face. Some of the smaller pebbles and dust obviously went into Brickman's eyes, because he yelled out and cursed, and began to brush the dust out of his eyes with his free hand.

Billy Joe ran, heading blindly for the wooded area at the bottom of the slope. He slithered and slipped down the rocks and scree, throwing himself from side to side, zig-zagging as he moved to stop Brickman from getting a proper aim at him. All the time he kept a firm hold on the pistol. Once he had an opportunity he'd find out what had gone wrong with the pistol and maybe put it right. But right now, he had to get to somewhere safe.

He heard a shot, and a bullet ricocheted off the rocks near him. He threw himself the last few paces towards the cover of the woodland and trees, just as two more bullets smashed into the trees nearest him.

As he ran, Billy Joe thought about Jess disappearing off the edge of the overhang and falling into the valley below. It made him feel sick. If he hadn't been killed by the bullet, the fall would have killed him. He felt a surge of anger at the idea of Jess being killed. But at the same time he knew he had to concentrate on getting away before Brickman killed him too.

By now he was in the thickness of the trees, and he tripped over a tree root and tumbled to the ground. Behind him he could hear Brickman crashing through the bushes.

Lying on the ground, Billy Joe opened the firing chamber, and saw that the hammer had come down on an empty chamber last time he'd pulled the trigger. There were two bullets left in the pistol. Billy Joe made sure the next time he pulled the trigger, the hammer would come down on a live round.

He could hear Brickman treading his through the undergrowth, and then the sound stopped. Brickman was obviously waiting for Billy Joe to show.

Billy Joe struggled to his knees as quietly as he could, pistol in hand. He knew he'd have no chance in a face-to-face shoot-out against a killer like Brickman, but he had to try something. The only way would be to try and spot where Brickman was hiding, and ambush him.

Billy Joe couldn't see the cowboy, but he knew he was there, hiding amongst the trees and undergrowth, not far away from him. He guessed Brickman was standing listening, just the same way that Billy Joe was. Listening for a sound that would tell him where Billy Joe was. The crack of a twig underfoot, or a bird suddenly being startled and flying away.

Billy Joe slowly got up from his crouching position behind the tree, keeping pressed against the trunk the whole time to keep himself hidden. He held the pistol in both hands. It wasn't just that the pistol was heavy – Billy Joe's hands were shaking with fear. He clenched his teeth and tried desperately to stop the fear taking hold of him. He had to be steady. When he pointed the gun at Brickman and pulled the trigger, he had to make sure the gun was firm or he'd miss. And he had just two bullets left. Miss with them, and he was dead.

Cautiously, he peered out from behind the cover of the tree. There was no sign of Brickman. Maybe the gunman was coming in the opposite direction? Maybe he was just on the other side of the same tree?

Then Billy Joe heard a noise to his left: the soft pad of a boot treading on something. Brickman was there!

Billy Joe strained his eyes, peering through the undergrowth, and suddenly he saw a spot of black against the green. Brickman's black outfit. The man was crouched behind a bush. Billy Joe guessed he was waiting for Billy Joe to make a move.

I have to get him with the first bullet, thought Billy Joe. *If I miss, or just wound him, he'll know where I am and he'll shoot me.*

Carefully, slowly, Billy Joe lifted the gun and pointed it at the spot of black he could see through the leaves and branches of the bush. He couldn't see Brickman clearly, but he hoped that the bullet would go through the greenery and hit him.

The patch of black moved slightly behind the greenery of the bush, and then stopped. Billy Joe pointed the pistol, holding it as firmly and as level as he could, his finger on the trigger.

Suddenly there was the sound of crashing in the undergrowth and a small boy's voice yelled out 'Patch!'

Andy!

Billy Joe saw Brickman shift as the Marshal twisted to take aim at the small boy.

BANG!

The gun leapt in Billy Joe's hand as he fired.

Billy Joe heard Brickman swear angrily and loudly.

At the same time, the noise from the woods came to an end.

'Billy Joe!' yelled Andy in panic.

The tall figure of Brickman rose up from behind the bush, gun in hand, swinging round now to aim directly at Billy Joe.

BANG!

Billy Joe fired again, and this time Brickman stumbled, then crashed backwards and fell into a bush.

'Stay where you are, Andy!' ordered Billy Joe.

Billy Joe waited, gun ready, pointing at the place where Brickman lay. The cowboy wouldn't know that the chambers were empty. All Billy Joe could see were Brickman's boots.

Moving slowly, Billy Joe moved forward, gun trained on his target. Even without bullets, holding the gun made him feel safe when he was this close to his enemy. Brickman didn't move. He lay, sprawled, eyes and mouth wide open, his pistol beside his hand. Both Billy Joe's bullets had hit him. There were two wounds on his body, one high on the shoulder, the second where his heart was. He was dead.

'Billy Joe?' called Andy.

'It's OK, Andy!' Billy Joe called. 'You just stay there!'

But Andy had already appeared, pushing his way through the undergrowth. He looked down at the body of Brickman.

'Is he dead?' he asked in a small voice.

Billy Joe nodded.

'Yep,' he said.

The triumph of shooting Brickman brought home that Jess was dead. It was revenge: a life for a life, but he'd rather his friend was still alive. His *best* friend.

There was the sound of barking, then Patch appeared.

'There you are, Patch!' yelled the delighted Andy. The dog rushed to Andy and leapt up at him, and Andy knelt down and hugged the dog, while Patch licked the small boy's face.

Suddenly Billy Joe remembered Mack, the gunman, in the valley.

'Where's the other gunman, Andy?' he demanded. 'The one who was gonna shoot you?'

'Jess has got him,' said Andy. 'He was tying him up when Patch ran off . . .'

'Jess?!' said Bill Joe, stunned.

Andy carried on fussing Patch.

'Uh-huh. He fell off that cliff but he hit an outcrop just below it, and he climbed down. Patch was still chewing on that gunman's arm, but Jess called Patch off and then he held the man's gun on him while I tied his feet together. I did real good job of tyin' up, Jess said,' he added proudly.

Jess was alive! A huge feeling of relief swept over Billy Joe.

'Let's go find him and tell him Brickman's dead!' he said.

With Andy and Patch close behind, Billy Joe ran through the undergrowth, pushing his way past bushes and branches, until he came to the narrow entrance to the valley.

Jess was crouched down near the trussed-up body of Mack, pointing the gunman's own pistol at him as the man came round.

'Jess!' yelled Billy Joe delightedly.

'Billy Joe!' called back Jess, relief on his face. 'I thought Brickman would have killed you!'

Billy Joe shook his head.

'No,' he said. Then he added, 'He's dead. I shot him.'

There was a pause, then Jess nodded once. 'You had to do it, Billy Joe. He didn't give you no choice.'

Billy Joe looked around for Mayor Redding, but there was no sign of him.

'Where's Mayor Redding?' he asked.

'He took off as soon as Patch started biting this guy here,' said Jess.

'I need a doctor!' moaned Mack, writhing with the pain from his chewed arm.

Suddenly they heard the sound of horses' hooves approaching fast.

'Brickman's men!' yelled Jess, and he and Billy Joe swung round, pistols aimed at the narrow entrance in the rocks.

But the first man through the entrance, riding hard, was Sheriff Nolan, gun drawn ready to use. Behind him came a posse of men, and with them was Shane.

Billy Joe and Jess lowered their guns and smiled at one another.

It was over.

CHAPTER 26

At the Johnsons' house in Drygulch, Jess, Billy Joe, Shane and Andy stood with Mr and Mrs Amberson and Jack by the bed where Manda was propped up against a pile of pillows. Patch had been tied up outside to make sure he didn't try and jump up on the bed where Manda lay.

Manda don't look bad for someone we thought was dying, mused Billy Joe.

Manda did, indeed, look better. She was still pale, but there was some colour in her cheeks. And she smiled as she looked at the boys.

'Doc Benson says the blood didn't come directly from her lungs. It was a build-up of blood in her stomach,' explained Mrs Amberson. 'She'd been swallowing it instead of spitting it out. He reckons she'll be all right now.'

Manda smiled and nodded, and wrote on her slate

'I'm going to get better.' Shane read the words aloud for the other boys.

'Well, that sure is good news,' said Jess.

A gentle tap at the door made them all look round. Sheriff Nolan was standing in the doorway.

'Sorry to interrupt,' he said. 'But there's someone outside would like a word.'

'Who is it?' asked Mrs Amberson.

'It's Colonel McVie.'

Immediately Mrs Amberson's face turned to stone.

'That man is not welcome here!' she said firmly.

'Indeed he isn't!' growled Amberson. 'The only time I want to see that man is in court for what he did!'

Nolan hesitated, then he said: 'I've been talking to both the Colonel, and to Brickman's man, Mack It seems that the Colonel didn't know what Brickman was really up to.'

'Then the man's a fool!' snapped Amberson.

'Yes he is,' agreed Nolan. 'And he'd like to tell you that himself.'

There was a difficult pause as Mr Amberson looked towards his wife. Finally, she nodded.

'You'd better go and see what he has to say, William,' she said.

Amberson nodded, and headed for the door. The boys could see from the grim expression on his face that he was in no mood to start believing or forgiving McVie.

'The Colonel would also like to talk to the boys,' added Nolan. 'If they don't mind.'

'Now?' asked Jess.

The Sheriff raised his eyebrows.

'He said what he has to say needs to be said out in the open so you can all hear,' he said.

The boys exchanged looks.

'OK,' Jess said. 'Let's go hear what he's got to say.'

The boys and Mr Amberson trooped outside the house. McVie was standing on the boardwalk, waiting for them. It was pretty obvious to Billy Joe that he looked very uncomfortable.

'Mr Amberson,' he tipped his hat in greeting. 'Boys.' He took a deep breath, then said: 'I owe you all an apology. I believed the things that Marshal Brickman told me about Adam Holtz and you taking my cattle. I now know that was not the case. I am truly sorry.'

'Being sorry won't bring back Adam Holtz!' snapped Amberson sharply.

McVie lowered his head.

'I know,' he said. 'And for that I am especially sorry. I've made arrangements to pay compensation to his widow, Dorcas. And to help her build up her homestead if she chooses to come out here after all.'

Jess shot McVie a puzzled look.

'You're sayin' she can come out and run her cattle here on this range and you won't interfere?' he asked, suspiciously.

McVie nodded.

'I've been forced to realise that things change. This land is not mine. I came out here and tamed it, but I'll never own it. No one will. The only proper way is to work together on it, and that means to share it.'

'So our fences . . . ?' began Amberson, taken aback.

'I was wrong, Mr Amberson,' said McVie. 'I hired a man I thought was a lawman to protect my interests, and he stole from me, and committed murder in my name. I have to try and make things right.

'I'm a rich man, made rich from cattle. So I offer you my hand as a neighbour, and my money to help you get started. I'm prepared to pay for the hire of some cowboys, decent ones this time, to get your place and your herd up and running. What do you say?'

Amberson looked stunned. He stared at Nolan, the expression on his face asking for confirmation. Nolan nodded.

'The Colonel's made that promise to me, and he's prepared to put it in writin',' confirmed Nolan. 'The range will be shared. You can fence it, or leave it open. But he suggests forming a Cattle Association where you work together.'

'It could be useful when it comes to movin' your cattle north to the stockyards of Chicago,' added McVie. 'The cattle trail is long and hard. Moving the herds together, with our men ridin' herd together on the way, could help us all.'

Amberson hesitated before he nodded.

'Yes, Colonel, I believe it could.'

'Then will you take my hand as a neighbour and, I hope, a future friend, and accept my apology?' asked McVie.

And he held out his right hand towards Amberson.

For a moment Amberson did nothing, then he took McVie's hand in his and shook it.

'I believe I will, Colonel,' he said.

McVie smiled.

'Thank you,' he said. 'Please extend an invitation to your wife and children to come and visit me as soon as your daughter is well enough to travel.'

'What about Mayor Redding?' piped up Andy. 'Is he gonna be arrested, Sheriff?'

Billy Joe looked at Jess and smiled. *Tell it like it is, Andy*, he thought.

'The Mayor says he just happened to be in the wrong place at the wrong time, Andy,' said Nolan, shaking his head. 'He didn't know the cattle he was going to buy were stolen. He had an offer to buy some cattle very cheap, and thought it was a good investment opportunity for the bank's customers.'

'And you believe that, Sheriff?' demanded Billy Joe.

Nolan shrugged.

'Nothin' that Mack told me contradicts that,' he said. 'He says that Brickman was the only one behind it all.'

'Th-this ain't f-fair!' blurted out Shane.

'It's not about fair, it's about the Law and havin' evidence against the Mayor . . .' began Nolan, but Shane cut him off.

'Not about the M-Mayor,' he said. 'Ab-bout us. We had s-somewhere to l-live and w-w-work at the Ambersons. If the Colonel g-gets c-cowboys they w-won't need us n-no more.'

'That's not true, Shane,' said Mr Amberson. 'As far as I'm concerned you can stay living with us, and working with us.'

'Although you may not need to,' said Nolan.

The boys looked at the Sheriff in surprise.

'What do you mean, Sheriff?' asked Billy Joe.

'I'll let the Colonel tell you himself,' said Nolan.

The boys turned their attention to McVie.

'As well as treatin' the Ambersons badly, I treated you boys badly,' he said. 'I was rude to you, and my men nearly killed you.'

'That's true,' said Jess, watching the Colonel closely.

'Also, if it hadn't been for you boys findin' out who the real rustlers were, I'd have carried on losin' cattle. You boys saved me a great deal, both in money and showin' me what the truth was.'

'We sure did!' said Andy firmly.

McVie nodded, hiding a smile, then continued, 'I understand that you lost your home a short while ago.'

'Yes, the Mayor stole it from us!' burst out Andy.

'He didn't steal it, Andy. He was taking it back,' said Nolan.

'That may be, but he th-threw us out without a w-warnin'!' said Shane angrily.

'Anyhow, I've bought a piece of land here in town and I'm going to have a small house built on it. Nothing grand, but it will do. I'm giving it to you boys as a gift to say thank you.'

The four boys stared at McVie, then at each other, stunned.

'A house?' echoed Jess.

'Of our own?' asked Billy Joe, still trying to get his head round this idea.

McVie nodded.

'W-where?' asked Shane.

'It's on one of the roads at the back of town,' said McVie.

Nolan smiled. 'It's the patch of land that Mayor Redding owned that had three old shacks on it,' he said. 'You may remember it.'

Billy Joe looked at Nolan's twinkling eyes, and then at Jess, Shane and Andy, a broad grin lighting up his face.

'It's where our old place was!' he said.

Slowly, a smile spread across Jess's face.

'Is that right, Sheriff?' he asked.

Nolan nodded, grinning from under the brim of his hat.

'I've arranged for men to come and start work the day after tomorrow,' McVie told them. 'It'll take a while. But it'll be a good house. Good walls. No leaks in the roof.'

'Until then, you're welcome to stay with us,' Mr Amberson told the boys.

Jess smiled again, broadly.

'That'll be right good, Mr Amberson,' he said. 'We'd love to.'

Billy Joe suddenly let out a whoop of delight and slapped Shane and Jess on the shoulders.

'Boys,' he grinned happily, 'we're goin' home!'

Look out for more BADLANDS books
by Eldridge James . . .

BADLANDS
DEATH IN DRYGULCH

ELDRIDGE JAMES

BADLANDS
DEATH IN DRYGULCH
ELDRIDGE JAMES

Discover why Billy Joe came to Drygulch and how he became one of the gang . . .

There were shouts and screams from both inside and outside the saloon, but Billy Joe was already running as fast as he could. Then there was another gunshot and he felt this bullet tear at his jacket. The next one would blow him apart.

Billy Joe saw his father being gunned down. Now the killers are after him.

The Drygulch gang have promised to save him but they're only boys. Can they really protect him from a ruthless band of desperadoes? His life depends on it!

BADLANDS
GOLD RUSH

BANG!

Billy Joe Ford froze in his tracks as the gunshot echoed through the night. It could have been one of the prospectors shooting at possum or a coyote, but the boy knew in his bones that it wasn't.

Hunters usually fired more than once.

A single shot meant one thing: a gunman.

When gold is discovered near Drygluch, people come from far and wide to cash in on the find. But greed can make men do dangerous things and it isn't long before bullets start to fly – with the gang caught in the middle.

NEXT IN THE EXCITING BADLANDS SERIES BY
ELDRIDGE JAMES